I0648007

# By Reef and Palm

*Louis Becke*

# Contents

# BY REEF AND PALM

BY

Louis Becke

# INTRODUCTION

When in October, 1870, I sailed into the harbour of Apia, Samoa, in the ill-fated ALBATROSS, Mr Louis Becke was gaining his first experiences of island life as a trader on his own account by running a cutter between Apia and Savai'i.

It was rather a notable moment in Apia, for two reasons. In the first place, the German traders were shaking in their shoes for fear of what the French squadron might do to them, and we were the bearers of the good news from Tahiti that the chivalrous Admiral Clouet, with a very proper magnanimity, had decided not to molest them; and, secondly, the beach was still seething with excitement over the departure on the previous day of the pirate Pease, carrying with him the yet more illustrious "Bully" Hayes.

It happened in this wise. A month or two before our arrival, Hayes had dropped anchor in Apia, and some ugly stories of recent irregularities in the labour trade had come to the ears of Mr Williams, the English Consul. Mr Williams, with the assistance of the natives, very cleverly seized his vessel in the night, and ran her ashore, and detained Mr Hayes pending the arrival of an English man-of-war to which he could be given in charge. But in those happy days there were no prisons in Samoa, so that his confinement was not irksome, and his only hard labour was picnics, of which he was the life and soul. All went pleasantly until Mr Pease--a degenerate sort of pirate who made his living by half bullying, half swindling lonely white men on small islands out of their coconut oil, and unarmed merchantmen out of their stores--came to Apia in an armed ship with a Malay crew. From that moment Hayes' life became less idyllic. Hayes and Pease conceived a most violent hatred of each other, and poor old Mr Williams was really worried into an attack of elephantiasis (which answers to the gout in those latitudes) by his continual efforts to prevent the two desperadoes from flying at each other's throat. Heartily glad was he when Pease--who was the sort of man that always observed LES CONVENANCES when possible, and who fired a salute of twenty-one guns on the Queen's Birthday--came one afternoon to get his papers "all regular," and clear for sea. But lo! the next morning, when his vessel had disappeared, it was found that his enemy Captain Hayes had disappeared also, and the ladies of Samoa were left disconsolate at the departure of the most agreeable man they had ever known.

However, all this is another story, as Mr Kipling says, and one which I hope Mr Becke will tell us more fully some day, for he knew Hayes well, having acted as supercargo on board his ship, and shared a shipwreck and other adventures with him.

But even before this date Mr Becke had had as much experience as falls to most men of adventures in the Pacific Ocean.

Born at Port Macquarrie in Australia, where his father was clerk of petty sessions, he was seized at the age of fourteen with an intense longing to go to sea. It is possible that he inherited this passion through his mother, for her father, Charles Beilby, who was private secretary to the Duke of Cumberland, invested a legacy that fell to him in a small vessel, and sailed with his family to the then very new world of Australia. However this may be, it was impossible to keep Louis Becke at home; and, as an alternative, a uncle undertook to send him, and a brother two years older, to a mercantile house in California. His first voyage was a terrible one. There were no steamers, of course, in those days, and they sailed for San Francisco in a wretched old barque. For over a month they were drifting about the stormy sea between Australia and New Zealand, a partially dismasted and leaking wreck. The crew mutinied--they had bitter cause to--and only after calling at Rurutu, in the Tubuai Group, and obtaining fresh food, did they permit the captain to resume command of the half-sunken old craft. They were ninety days in reaching Honolulu, and another forty in making the Californian coast.

The two lads did not find the routine of a merchant's office at all to their taste; and while the elder obtained employment on a sheep ranche at San Juan, Louis, still faithful to the sea, got a berth as a clerk in a steamship company, and traded to the Southern ports. In a year's time he had money enough to take passage in a schooner bound on a shark-catching cruise to the equatorial islands of the North

Pacific. The life was a very rough one, and full of incident and adventure--which I hope he will relate some day. Returning to Honolulu, he fell in with an old captain who had bought a schooner for a trading venture amongst the Western Carolines. Becke put in $1000, and sailed with him as supercargo, he and the skipper being the only white men on board. He soon discovered that, though a good seaman, the old man knew nothing of navigation. In a few weeks they were among the Marshall Islands, and the captain went mad from DELIRIUM TREMENS. Becke and the three native sailors ran the vessel into a little uninhabited atoll, and for a week had to keep the captain tied up to prevent his killing himself. They got him right at last, and stood to the westward. On their voyage they were witnesses of a tragedy (in this instance fortunately not complete), on which the pitiless sun of the Pacific has looked down very often. They fell in with a big Marshall Island sailing canoe that had been blown out of sight of land, and had drifted six hundred miles to the westward. Out of her complement of fifty people, thirty were dead. They gave them provisions and water, and left them to make Strong's Island (Kusaie), which was in sight. Becke and the chief swore Marshall Island BRUDERSCHAFT with each other. Years afterwards, when he came to live in the Marshall Group, the chief proved his friendship in a signal manner.

The cruise proved a profitable one, and from that time Mr Becke determined to become a trader, and to learn to know the people of the north-west Pacific; and returning to California, he made for Samoa, and from thence to Sydney. But at this time the Palmer River gold rush had just broken out in North Queensland, and a brother, who was a bank manager on the celebrated Charters Towers goldfields, invited him to come up, as every one seemed to be making his fortune. He wandered between the rushes for two years, not making a fortune, but acquiring much useful experience, learning, amongst other things, the art of a blacksmith, and becoming a crack shot with a rifle. Returning to Sydney, he sailed for the Friendly Islands (Tonga) in company with the king of Tonga's yacht--the TAUFAAHAU. The Friendly Islanders disappointed him (at which no one that knows them will wonder), and he went on to Samoa, and set up as a trader on his own account for the first time. He and a Manhiki half-caste--the "Allan" who so frequently figures in his stories--bought a cutter, and went trading throughout the group. This was the time of Colonel Steinberger's brief tenure of power. The natives were fighting, and the cut-

ter was seized on two occasions. When the war was over he made a voyage to the
north-west, and became a great favourite with the natives, as indeed seems to have
been the case in most of the places he went to in Polynesia and Micronesia. Later on
he was sent away from Samoa in charge of a vessel under sealed orders to the Marshall Islands. These orders were to hand the vessel over to the notorious Captain
"Bully" Hayes. (Some day he promises that he will give us the details of this very
curious adventure). He found Hayes awaiting him in his famous brig LEONORA in
Milli Lagoon. He handed over his charge and took service with him as supercargo.
After some months' cruising in the Carolines they were wrecked on Strong's Island
(Kusaie). Hayes made himself the ruler of the island, and Mr Becke and he had a
bitter quarrel. The natives treated the latter with great kindness, and gave him land
on the lee side of the island, where he lived happily enough for five months. Hayes
was captured by an English man-of-war, but escaped and went to Guam. Mr Becke
went back in the cruiser to the Colonies, and then again sailed for Eastern Polynesia, trading in the Gambiers, Paumotus, and Easter and Pitcairn Islands. In this part
of the ocean he picked up an abandoned French barque on a reef, floated her, and
loaded her with coconuts, intending to sail her to New Zealand with a native crew,
but they went ashore in a hurricane and lost everything. Meeting with Mr Tom de
Wolf, the managing partner of a Liverpool firm, he took service with him as a trader
in the Ellice and Tokelau Groups, finally settling down as a residential trader. Then
he took passage once more for the Carolines, and was wrecked on Peru, one of the
Gilbert Islands (lately annexed), losing every dollar that he possessed. He returned
to Samoa and engaged as a "recruiter" in the labour trade. He got badly hurt in an
encounter with some natives, and went to New Zealand to recover. Then he sailed
to New Britain on a trading venture, and fell in with, and had much to do with,
the ill-fated colonising expedition of the Marquis de Ray in New Ireland. A bad attack of malarial fever, and a wound in the neck (labour recruiting or even trading
among the blacks of Melanesia seems to have been a much less pleasant business
than residence among the gentle brown folk of the Eastern Pacific) made him leave
and return to the Marshall Islands, where Lailik, the chief whom he had succoured
at sea years before, made him welcome. He left on a fruitless quest after an imagi-
nary guano island, and from then until two years ago he has been living on various
islands in both the North and South Pacific, leading what he calls "a wandering and

lonely but not unhappy existence," "Lui," as they call him, being a man both liked and trusted by the natives from lonely Easter Island to the faraway Pelews. He is still in the prime of life, and whether he will now remain within the bounds of civilisation, or whether some day he will return to his wanderings, as Odysseus is fabled to have done in his old age, I fancy that he hardly knows himself. But when once the charm of a wild roving life has got into a man's blood, the trammels of civilisation are irksome and its atmosphere is hard to breathe. It will be seen from this all-too-condensed sketch of Mr Becke's career that he knows the Pacific as few men alive or dead have ever known it. He is one of the rare men who have led a very wild life, and have the culture and talent necessary to give some account of it. As a rule, the men who know don't write, and the men who write don't know.

Every one who has a taste for good stories will feel, I believe, the force of these. Every one who knows the South Seas, and, I believe, many who do not, will feel that they have the unmistakable stamp of truth. And truth to nature is a great merit in a story, not only because of that thrill of pleasure hard to analyse, but largely made up of associations, memories, and suggestions that faithfulness of representation in picture or book gives to the natural man; but because of the fact that nature is almost infinitely rich, and the unassisted imagination of man but a poor and sterile thing, tending constantly towards some ossified convention. "Treasure Island" is a much better story than "The Wreckers," yet I, for one, shall never cease to regret that Mr Stevenson did not possess, when he wrote "Treasure Island," that knowledge of what men and schooners do in wild seas that was his when he gave us "The Wreckers." The detail would have been so much richer and more convincing.

It is open to any one to say that these tales are barbarous, and what Mrs Meynell, in a very clever and amusing essay, has called "decivilised." Certainly there is a wide gulf separating life on a Pacific island from the accumulated culture of centuries of civilisation in the midst of which such as Mrs Meynell move and have their being. And if there can be nothing good in literature that does not spring from that culture, these stories must stand condemned. But such a view is surely too narrow. Much as I admire that lady's writings, I never can think of a world from which everything was eliminated that did not commend itself to the dainty taste of herself and her friends, without a feeling of impatience and suffocation. It takes a huge variety of men and things to make a good world. And ranches and CANONS, veldts and prairies, tropical forests and coral islands, and all that goes to make up the wild life in the face of Nature or among primitive races, far and free from the artificial conditions of an elaborate civilisation, form an element in the world, the loss of which would be bitterly felt by many a man who has never set foot outside his native land.

There is a certain monotony, perhaps, about these stories. To some extent this is inevitable. The interest and passions of South Sea Island life are neither numerous nor complex, and action is apt to be rapid and direct. A novelist of that modern school that fills its volumes, often fascinatingly enough, by refining upon the shadowy refinements of civilised thought and feeling, would find it hard to ply his trade in South Sea Island society. His models would always be cutting short in five minutes the hesitations and subtleties that ought to have lasted them through a quarter of a life-time. But I think it is possible that the English reader might gather from this little book an unduly strong impression of the uniformity of Island life. The loves of white men and brown women, often cynical and brutal, sometimes exquisitely tender and pathetic, necessarily fill a large space in any true picture of the South Sea Islands, and Mr Becke, no doubt of set artistic purpose, has confined himself in the collection of tales now offered almost entirely to this facet of the life. I do not question that he is right in deciding to detract nothing from the striking effect of these powerful stories, taken as a whole, by interspersing amongst them others of a different character. But I hope it may be remembered that the present selection is only an instalment, and that, if it finds favour with the British public, we may expect from him some of those tales of adventure, and of purely native life and custom, which no one could tell so well as he.

## PEMBROKE.
## CHALLIS THE DOUBTER
### The White Lady And The Brown Woman

Four years had come and gone since the day that Challis, with a dull and savage misery in his heart, had, cursing the love-madness which once possessed him, walked out from his house in an Australian city with an undefined and vague purpose of going "somewhere" to drown his sense of wrong and erase from his memory the face of the woman who, his wife of not yet a year, had played with her honour and his. So he thought, anyhow.

\* \* \* \*

You see, Challis was "a fool"--at least so his pretty, violet-eyed wife had told him that afternoon with a bitter and contemptuous ring in her voice when he had brought another man's letter--written to her--and with impulsive and jealous haste had asked her to explain. He was a fool, she had said, with an angry gleam in the violet eyes, to think she could not "take care" of herself. Admit receiving that letter? Of course! Did he think she could help other men writing silly letters to her? Did he not think she could keep out of a mess? And she smiled the self-satisfied smile of a woman conscious of many admirers and of her own powers of intrigue.

Then Challis, with a big effort, gulping down the rage that stirred him, made his great mistake. He spoke of his love for her. Fatuity! She laughed at him, said that as she detested women, his love was too exacting for her, if it meant that she should never be commonly friendly with any other man.

\* \* \* \*

Challis looked at her steadily for a few moments, trying to smother the wild flood of black suspicion aroused in him by the discovery of the letter, and confirmed by her sneering words, and then said quietly, but with a dangerous inflection in his voice--

"Remember--you are my wife. If you have no regard for your own reputation, you shall have some for mine. I don't want to entertain my friends by thrashing R----, but I'm not such a fool as you think. And if you go further in this direction you'll find me a bit of a brute."

Again the sneering laugh--"Indeed! Something very tragic will occur, I suppose?"

"No," said Challis grimly, "something damned prosaic--common enough among men with pretty wives--I'll clear out."

"I wish you would do that now," said his wife, "I hate you quite enough."

Of course she didn't quite mean it. She really liked Challis in her own small-souled way--principally because his money had given her the social pleasures denied her during her girlhood. With an unmoved face and without farewell he left her and went to his lawyer's.

A quarter of an hour later he arose to go, and the lawyer asked him when he intended returning.

"That all depends upon her. If she wants me back again, she can write, through you, and I'll come--if she has conducted herself with a reasonable amount of propriety for such a pretty woman."

Then, with an ugly look on his face, Challis went out; next day he embarked in the LADY ALICIA for a six months' cruise among the islands of the North-west Pacific.

* * * *

That was four years ago, and to-day Challis, who stands working at a little table set in against an open window, hammering out a ring from a silver coin on a marline-spike and vyce, whistles softly and contentedly to himself as he raises his head and glances through the vista of coconuts that surround his dwelling on this lonely and almost forgotten island.

"The devil!" he thinks to himself, "I must be turning into a native. Four years! What an ass I was! And I've never written yet--that is, never sent a letter away. Well, neither has she. Perhaps, after all, there was little in that affair of R----'s. . . . By God! though, if there was, I've been very good to them in leaving them a clear field. Anyhow, she's all right as regards money. I'm glad I've done that. It's a big prop to a man's conscience to feel he hasn't done anything mean; and she likes money--most women do. Of course I'll go back--if she writes. If not--well, then, these sinful islands can claim me for their own; that is, Nalia can."

* * * *

A native boy with shaven head, save for a long tuft on the left side, came down from the village, and, seating himself on the gravelled space inside the fence, gazed at the white man with full, lustrous eyes.

"Hallo, TAMA!" said Challis, "whither goest now?"

"Pardon, Tialli. I came to look at thee making the ring. Is it of soft silver--and for Nalia, thy wife?"

"Ay, O shaven-head, it is. Here, take this MASI and go pluck me a young nut to drink," and Challis threw him a ship-biscuit. Then he went on tapping the little band of silver. He had already forgotten the violet eyes, and was thinking with almost childish eagerness of the soft glow in the black orbs of Nalia when she should see his finished handiwork.

The boy returned with a young coconut, unhusked. "Behold, Tialli. This nut is a UTO GA'AU (sweet husk). When thou hast drunk the juice give it me back, that I may chew the husk which is sweet as the sugar-cane of Samoa," and he squatted down again on the gravel.

* * * *

Challis drank, then threw him the husk and resumed his work. Presently the boy, tearing off a strip of the husk with his white teeth, said, "Tialli, how is it that there be no drinking-nuts in thy house?"

"Because, O turtle-head, my wife is away; and there are no men in the village to-day; and because the women of this MOTU [Island or country.] I have no thought that the PAPALAGI [Foreigner] may be parched with thirst, and so come not near me with a coconut." This latter in jest.

"Nay, Tialli. Not so. True it is that to-day all the men are in the bush binding FALA leaves around the coconut trees, else do the rats steal up and eat the buds and clusters of little nuts. And because Nalia, thy wife, is away at the other White Man's house no woman cometh inside the door."

Challis laughed. "O evil-minded people of Nukunono! And must I, thy PAPALAGI, be parched with thirst because of this?"

"FAIAGA OE, Tialli, thou but playest with me. Raise thy hand and call out 'I thirst!' and every woman in the village will run to thee, each with a drinking-nut, and those that desire thee, but are afraid, will give two. But to come inside when Nalia is away would be to put shame on her."

* * * *

The white man mused. The boy's solemn chatter entertained him. He knew well the native customs; but, to torment the boy, he commenced again.

"O foolish custom! See how I trust my wife Nalia. Is she not even now in the house of another white man?"

"True. But, then, he is old and feeble, and thou young and strong. None but a fool desires to eat a dried flying-fish when a fresh one may be had."

"O wise man with the shaven crown," said Challis, with mocking good nature, "thou art full of wisdom of the ways of women. And if I were old and withered, would Nalia then be false to me in a house of another and younger white man?"

"How could she? Would not he, too, have a wife who would watch her? And if he had not, and were NOFO NOA (single), would he be such a fool to steal that the like of which he can buy--for there are many girls without husbands as good to look on as that Nalia of thine. And all women are alike," and then, hearing a woman's voice calling his name, he stood up.

"Farewell, O ULU TULA POTO (Wise Baldhead)," said Challis, as the boy, still chewing his sweet husk, walked back to the native houses clustered under the grove of PUA trees.

\* \* \* \*

Ere dusk, Nalia came home, a slenderly-built girl with big dreamy eyes, and a heavy mantle of wavy hair. A white muslin gown, fastened at the throat with a small silver brooch, was her only garment, save the folds of the navy-blue-and-white LAVA LAVA round her waist, which the European-fashioned garment covered.

Challis was lying down when she came in. Two girls who came with her carried baskets of cooked food, presents from old Jack Kelly, Challis's fellow-trader. At a sign from Nalia the girls took one of the baskets of food and went away. Then, taking off her wide-brimmed hat of FALA leaf, she sat down beside Challis and pinched his cheek.

"O lazy one! To let me walk from the house of Tiaki all alone!"

"Alone! There were two others with thee."

"Tapa Could I talk to THEM! I, a white man's wife, must not be too familiar with every girl, else they would seek to get presents from me with sweet words. Besides, could I carry home the fish and cooked fowl sent thee by old Tiaki? That would be unbecoming to me, even as it would be if thou climbed a tree for a coconut,"--and the daughter of the Tropics laughed merrily as she patted Challis on his sunburnt cheek.

Challis rose, and going to a little table, took from it the ring.

"See, Nalia, I am not lazy as thou sayest. This is thine."

The girl with an eager "AUE!" took the bauble and placed it on her finger. She made a pretty picture, standing there in the last glow of the sun as it sank into the ocean, her languorous eyes filled with a tender light.

Challis, sitting on the end of the table regarding her with half-amused interest as does a man watching a child with a toy, suddenly flushed hotly. "By God! I can't be such a fool as to begin to LOVE her in reality, but yet . . . Come here, Nalia," and he drew her to him, and, turning her face up so that he might look into her eyes, he asked:

"Nalia, hast thou ever told me any lies?"

The steady depths of those dark eyes looked back into his, and she answered:

"Nay, I fear thee too much to lie. Thou mightst kill me."

"I do but ask thee some little things. It matters not to me what the answer is. Yet see that thou keepest nothing hidden from me."

The girl, with parted lips and one hand on his, waited.

"Before thou became my wife, Nalia, hadst thou any lovers?"

"Yes, two--Kapua and Tafu-le-Afi."

"And since?"

"May I choke and perish here before thee if I lie! None."

Challis, still holding her soft brown chin in his hand, asked her one more question--a question that only one of his temperament would have dared to ask a girl of the Tokelaus.

"Nalia, dost thou love me?"

"Aye, ALOFA TUMAU (everlasting love). Am I a fool? Are there not Letia, and Miriami, and Eline, the daughter of old Tiaki, ready to come to this house if I love any but thee? Therefore my love is like the suckers of the FA'E (octopus) in its strength. My mother has taught me much wisdom."

A curious feeling of satisfaction possessed the man, and next day Letia, the "show" girl of the village, visiting Challis's store to buy a tin of salmon, saw Nalia, the Lucky One, seated on a mat beneath the seaward side of the trader's house, surrounded by a billowy pile of yellow silk, diligently sewing.

"Ho, dear friend of my heart! Is that silken dress for thee? For the love of God, let me but touch it. Four dollars a fathom it be priced at. Thy husband is indeed the king of generosity. Art thou to become a mother?"

"Away, silly fool, and do thy buying and pester me not."

* * * *

Challis, coming to the corner of the house, leant against a post, and something white showed in his hand. It was a letter. His letter to the woman of violet eyes, written a week ago, in the half-formed idea of sending it some day. He read it through, and then paused and looked at Nalia. She raised her head and smiled. Slowly, piece by piece, he tore it into tiny little squares, and, with a dreamy hand-wave, threw them away. The wind held them in mid-air for a moment, and then carried the little white flecks to the beach.

"What is it?" said the bubbling voice of Letia, the Disappointed.

"Only a piece of paper that weighed as a piece of iron on my bosom. But it is gone now."

"Even so," said Letia, smelling the gaudy label on the tin of salmon in the anticipative ecstasy of a true Polynesian, "PE SE MEA FA'AGOTOIMOANA (like a thing buried deep in ocean). May God send me a white man as generous as thee--a whole tin of SAMANI for nothing! Now do I know that Nalia will bear thee a son."

* * * *

And that is why Challis the Doubter has never turned up again.

# "'TIS IN THE BLOOD"

**W**e were in Manton's Hotel at Levuka-Levuka in her palmy days. There were Robertson, of the barque ROLUMAH; a fat German planter from the Yasawa Group; Harry the Canadian, a trader from the Tokelaus, and myself.

Presently a knock came to the door, and Allan, the boatswain of our brig, stood hat in hand before us. He was a stalwart half-caste of Manhiki, and, perhaps, the greatest MANAIA (Lothario) from Ponape to Fiji.

"Captain say to come aboard, please. He at the Consul's for papers--he meet you at boat," and Allan left.

"By shingo, dot's a big fellow," said Planter Oppermann.

"Ay," said Robertson, the trading skipper, "and a good man with his mauleys, too. He's the champion knocker-out in Samoa, and is a match for any Englishman in Polynesia, let alone foreigners"--with a sour glance at the German.

"Well, good-bye all," I said. "I'm sorry, Oppermann, I can't stay for another day for your wedding, but our skipper isn't to be got at anyhow."

The trading captain and Harry walked with me part of the way, and then began the usual Fiji GUP.

"Just fancy that fat-headed Dutchman going all the way to Samoa and picking on a young girl and sending her to the Sisters to get educated properly! As if any old beach-girl isn't good enough for a blessed Dutchman. Have you seen her?"

"No," I said; "Oppermann showed me her photo. Pretty girl. Says she's been three years with the Sisters in Samoa, and has got all the virtues of her white father, and none of the vices of her Samoan mammy. Told me he's spent over two thousand dollars on her already."

Robertson smiled grimly. "Ay, I don't doubt it. He's been all round Levuka cracking her up. I brought her here last week, and the Dutchman's been in a chronic state of silly ever since. She's an almighty fine girl. She's staying with the Sisters here till the marriage. By the Lord, here she is now coming along the street! Bet a dollar she's been round Vagadace way, where there are some fast Samoan women living. 'Tis in the blood, I tell you."

The future possessor of the Oppermann body and estate WAS a pretty girl. Only those who have seen fair young Polynesian half-castes--before they get married, and grow coarse, and drink beer, and smoke like a factory chimney--know how pretty.

Our boat was at the wharf, and just as we stood talking Allan sauntered up and asked me for a dollar to get a bottle of gin. Just then the German's FIANCEE reached us. Robertson introduced Harry and myself to her, and then said good-bye. She stood there in the broiling Fijian sun with a dainty sunshade over her face, looking so lovely and cool in her spotless muslin dress, and withal so innocent, that I no longer wondered at the Dutchman's "chronic state of silly."

Allan the Stalwart stood by waiting for his dollar. The girl laughed joyously when Harry the Canadian said he would be at the wedding and have a high time, and held out her soft little hand as he bade her adieu and strolled off for another drink.

The moment Harry had gone Allan was a new man. Pulling off his straw hat, he saluted her in Samoan, and then opened fire.

"There are many TEINE LALELEI (beautiful girls) in the world, but there is none so beautiful as thou. Only truth do I speak, for I have been to all countries of the world. Ask him who is here--our supercargo--if I lie. O maid with the teeth of pearl and face like FETUAO (the morning star), my stomach is drying up with the fire of love."

The sunshade came a little lower, and the fingers played nervously with the ivory handle. I leant against a coconut tree and listened.

"Thy name is Vaega. See that! How do I know? Aha, how do I? Because, for two years or more, whenever I passed by the stone wall of the Sisters' dwelling in Matafele, I climbed up and watched thee, O Star of the Morning, and I heard the other girls call thee Vaega. Oho! and some night I meant to steal thee away."

(The rascal! He told me two days afterwards that the only time he ever climbed the Mission wall was to steal mangoes.)

The sunshade was tilted back, and displayed two big, black eyes, luminous with admiring wonder.

"And so thou hast left Samoa to come here to be devoured by this fat hog of a Dutchman! Dost thou not know, O foolish, lovely one, that she who mates with a SIAMANI (German) grows old in quite a little time, and thy face, which is now smooth and fair, will be coarse as the rind of a half-ripe bread-fruit, because of the foul food these swine of Germans eat?"

"Allan," I called, "here's the captain!"

There was a quick clasp of hands as the Stalwart One and the Maid hurriedly spoke again, this time in a whisper, and then the white muslin floated away out of sight.

The captain was what he called "no' so dry"--viz. half-seas over, and very jolly. He told Allan he could have an hour to himself to buy what he wanted, and then told me that the captain of a steam collier had promised to give us a tug out at day-light. "I'm right for the wedding-feast after all," I thought.

* * * *

But the wedding never came off. That night Oppermann, in a frantic state, was tearing round Levuka hunting for his love, who had disappeared. At daylight, as the collier steamed ahead and tautened our tow-line, we could see the parties of searchers with torches scouring the beach. Our native sailors said they had heard a scream about ten at night and seen the sharks splashing, and the white liars of Levuka shook their heads and looked solemn as they told tales of monster sharks with eight-foot jaws always cruising close in to the shore at night.

* * * *

Three days afterwards Allan came to me with stolid face and asked for a bottle of wine, as Vaega was very sea-sick. I gave him the wine, and threatened to tell the captain. He laughed, and said he would fight any man, captain or no captain, who meddled with him. And, as a matter of fact, he felt safe--the skipper valued him too much to bully him over the mere stealing of a woman. So the limp and sea-sick Vaega was carried up out of the sweating foc'sle and given a cabin berth, and Allan planked down two twenty-dollar pieces for her passage to the Union Group. When she got better she sang rowdy songs, and laughed all day, and made fun of the holy Sisters. And one day Allan beat her with a deal board because she sat down on a band-box in the trade-room and ruined a hat belonging to a swell official's wife in Apia. And she liked him all the better for it.

* * * *

The fair Vaega was Mrs Allan for just six months, when his erratic fancy was captivated by the daughter of Mauga, the chief of Tutuila, and an elopement resulted to the mountains. The subsequent and inevitable parting made Samoa an undesirable place of residence for Allan, who shipped as boatsteerer in the NIGER of New Bedford. As for Vaega, she drifted back to Apia, and there, right under the shadow of the Mission Church, she flaunted her beauty. The last time I saw her was in Charley the Russian's saloon, when she showed me a letter. It was from the bereaved Oppermann, asking her to come back and marry him.

"Are you going?" I said.

"E PULE LE ATUA (if God so wills), but he only sent me twenty dollars, and that isn't half enough. However, there's an American man-of-war coming next week, and these other girls will see then. I'll make the PAPALAGI [foriegn] officers shell out. TO FA, ALII [Good-bye]."

## THE REVENGE OF MACY O'SHEA

## A Story Of The Marquesas
## I.

Tikena the Clubfooted guided me to an open spot in the jungle-growth, and, sitting down on the butt of a twisted TOA, indicated by a sweep of his tattooed arm the lower course of what had once been the White Man's dwelling.

"Like unto himself was this, his house," he said, puffing a dirty clay pipe, "square-built and strong. And the walls were of great blocks made of PANISINA-- of coral and lime and sand mixed together; and around each centre-post--posts that to lift one took the strength of fifty men--was wound two thousand fathoms of thin plaited cinnet, stained red and black. APA! he was a great man here in these MOTU (islands), although he fled from prison in your land; and when he stepped on the beach the marks of the iron bands that had once been round his ankles were yet red to the sight. There be none such as he in these days. But he is now in Hell."

This was the long-deferred funeral oration of Macy O'Shea, sometime member of the chain-gang of Port Arthur, in Van Dieman's Land, and subsequently runaway convict, beachcomber, cutter-off of whaleships, and Gentleman of Leisure in Eastern Polynesia. And of his many known crimes the deed done in this isolated spot was the darkest of all. Judge of it yourself.

\* \* \* \*

The arrowy shafts of sunrise had scarce pierced the deep gloom of the silent forest ere the village woke to life. Right beside the thatch-covered dwelling of Macy O'Shea, now a man of might, there towers a stately TAMANU tree; and, as the first faint murmur of women's voices arises from the native huts, there is a responsive twittering and cooing in the thickly-leaved branches, and further back in the forest the heavy, booming note of the red-crested pigeon sounds forth like the beat of a muffled drum.

\* \* \* \*

With slow, languid step, Sera, the wife of Macy O'Shea, comes to the open door and looks out upon the placid lagoon, now just rippling beneath the first breath of the trade-wind, and longs for courage to go out there--there to the point of the reef--and spring over among the sharks. The girl--she is hardly yet a woman--shudders a moment and passes her white hand before her eyes, and then, with a sudden gust of passion, the hand clenches. "I would kill him--kill him, if there was but a ship here in which I could get away! I would sell myself over and over again to the worst whaler's crew that ever sailed the Pacific if it would bring me freedom from this cruel, cold-blooded devil!"

\* \* \* \*

A heavy tread on the matted floor of the inner room and her face pales to the hue of death. But Macy O'Shea is somewhat shy of his two years' wife this morning, and she hears the heavy steps recede as he walks over to his oil-shed. A flock of GOGO cast their shadow over the lagoon as they fly westward, and the woman's eyes follow them--"Kill him, yes. I am afraid to die, but not to kill. And I am a stranger here, and if I ran a knife into his fat throat, these natives would make me work in the taro-fields, unless one wanted me for himself." Then the heavy step returns, and she slowly faces round to the blood-shot eyes and drink-distorted face of the man she hates, and raises one hand to her lips to hide a blue and swollen bruise.

The man throws his short, square-set figure on a rough native sofa, and, passing one brawny hand meditatively over his stubbly chin, says, in a voice like the snarl of a hungry wolf: "Here, I say, Sera, slew round; I want to talk to you, my beauty."

The pale, set face flushed and paled again. "What is it, Macy O'Shea?"

"Ho, ho, 'Macy O'Shea,' is it? Well, just this. Don't be a fool. I was a bit put about last night, else I wouldn't have been so quick with my fist. Cut your lip, I see. Well, you must forget it; any way, it's the first time I ever touched you. But you ought to know by now that I am not a man to be trifled with; no man, let alone a woman, is going to set a course for Macy O'Shea to steer by. And, to come to the point at once, I want you to understand that Carl Ristow's daughter is coming here. I want her, and that's all about it."

\* \* \* \*

The woman laughed scornfully. "Yes, I know. That was why"--she pointed to her lips. "Have you no shame? I know you have no pity. But listen. I swear to you by the Mother of Christ that I will kill her--kill you, if you do this."

O'Shea's cruel mouth twitched and his jaws set, then he uttered a hoarse laugh. "By God! Has it taken you two years to get jealous?"

A deadly hate gleamed in the dark, passionate eyes. "Jealous, Mother of God! jealous of a drunken, licentious wretch such as you! I hate you--hate you! If I had courage enough I would poison myself to be free from you."

O'Shea's eyes emitted a dull sparkle. "I wish you would, damn you! Yet you are game enough, you say, to kill me--and Malia?"

"Yes. But not for love of you, but because of the white blood in me. I can't--I won't be degraded by you bringing another woman here."

"'Por Dios,' as your dad used to say before the devil took his soul, we'll see about that, my beauty. I suppose because your father was a d----d garlic-eating, ear-ringed Dago, and your mother a come-by-chance Tahiti half-caste, you think he was as good as me."

"As good as you, O bloody-handed dog of an English convict. He was a man, and the only wrong he ever did was to let me become wife to a devil like you."

The cruel eyes were close to hers now, and the rough, brawny hands gripped her wrists. "You spiteful Portuguese quarter-bred ----! Call me a convict again, and I'll twist your neck like a fowl's. You she-devil! I'd have made things easy for you--but I won't now. Do you hear?" and the grip tightened. "Ristow's girl will be here to-morrow, and if you don't knuckle down to her it'll be a case of 'Vamos' for you--you can go and get a husband among the natives," and he flung her aside and went to the god that ran him closest for his soul, next to women--his rum-bottle.

* * * *

O'Shea kept his word, for two days later Malia, the half-caste daughter of Ristow, the trader at Ahunui, stepped from out her father's whaleboat in front of O'Shea's house. The transaction was a perfectly legitimate one, and Malia did not allow any inconvenient feeling of modesty to interfere with such a lucrative arrangement as this, whereby her father became possessed of a tun of oil and a bag of Chilian dollars, and she of much finery. In those days missionaries had not made much head-way, and gentlemen like Messrs Ristow and O'Shea took all the wind out of the Gospel drum.

And so Malia, dressed as a native girl, with painted cheeks and bare bosom, walked demurely up from the boat to the purchaser of her sixteen-years'-old beauty, who, with arms folded across his broad chest, stood in the middle of the path that led from the beach to his door. And within, with set teeth and a knife in the bosom of her blouse bodice, Sera panted with the lust of Hate and Revenge.

* * * *

The bulky form of O'Shea darkened the door-way. "Sera," he called in English, with a mocking, insulting inflection in his voice, "come here and welcome my new wife!"

Sera came, walking slowly, with a smile on her lips, and, holding out her left hand to Malia, said in the native language, "Welcome!"

"Why," said O'Shea, with mocking jocularity, "that's a left-handed welcome, Sera."

"Aye," said the girl with the White Man's blood, "my right hand is for this"--and the knife sank home into Malia's yellow bosom. "A cold bosom for you to-night, Macy O'Shea," she laughed, as the value of a tun of oil and a bag of Chilian dollars gasped out its life upon the matted floor.

# II

The native drum was beating. As the blood-quickening boom reverberated through the village, the natives came out from their huts and gathered around the House of the Old Men, where, with bound hands and feet, Sera, the White Man's wife, sat, with her back to one of the centre-posts. And opposite her, sitting like a native on a mat of KAPAU, was the burly figure of O'Shea, with the demon of disappointed passion eating away his reason, and a mist of blood swimming before his eyes.

The people all detested her, especially the soft-voiced, slender-framed women. In that one thing savages resemble Christians--the deadly hatred with which some women hate those of their sex whom they know to be better and more pure than themselves. So the matter was decided quickly. Mesi--so they called O'Shea--should have justice. If he thought death, let it be death for this woman who had let out the blood of his new wife. Only one man, Loloku the Boar Hunter, raised his voice for her, because Sera had cured him of a bad wound when his leg had been torn open by the tusk of a wild boar. But the dull glare from the eyes of O'Shea fell on him, and he said no more. Then at a sign from the old men the people rose from the mats, and two unbound the cords of AFA from the girl, and led her out into the square, and looked at O'Shea.

"Take her to the boat," he said.

\* \* \* \*

Ristow's boat had been hauled up, turned over, and covered with the rough mats called KAPAU to keep off the heat of the sun. With staggering feet, but undaunted heart, the girl Sera was led down. Only once she turned her head and looked back. Perhaps Loloku would try again. Then, as they came to the boat, a young girl, at a sign from O'Shea, took off the loose blouse, and they placed her, face downwards, across the bilge of the boat, and two pair of small, eager, brown hands each seized one of hers and dragged the white, rounded arms well over the keel of the boat. O'Shea walked round to that side, drawing through his hands the long, heavy, and serrated tail of the FAI--the gigantic stinging-ray of Oceana. He would have liked to wield it himself, but then he would have missed part of his revenge--he could not have seen her face. So he gave it to a native, and watched, with the smile of a fiend, the white back turn black and then into bloody red as it was cut to pieces with the tail of the FAI.

\* \* \* \*

The sight of the inanimate thing that had given no sign of its agony beyond the shudderings and twitchings of torn and mutilated flesh was, perhaps, disappointing to the tiger who stood and watched the dark stream that flowed down on both sides of the boat. Loloku touched his arm--"Mesi, stay thy hand. She is dead else."

"Ah," said O'Shea, "that would be a pity; for with one hand shall she live to plant taro."

And, hatchet in hand, he walked in between the two brown women who held her hands. They moved aside and let go. Then O'Shea swung his arm; the blade of the hatchet struck into the planking, and the right hand of Sera fell on the sand.

A man put his arms around her, and lifted her off the boat. He placed his hand on the blood-stained bosom and looked at Macy O'Shea.

"E MATE! [Dead!]" he said.

# THE RANGERS OF THE TIA KAU

Between Nanomea and Nanomaga--two of the Ellice Group--but within a few miles of the latter, is an extensive submerged shoal, on the charts called the Grand Cocal Reef, but by the people of the two islands known as Tia Kau (The Reef). On the shallowest part there are from four to ten fathoms of water, and here in heavy weather the sea breaks. The British cruiser BASILISK, about 1870, sought for the reef, but reported it as non-existent. Yet the Tia Kati is well known to many a Yankee whaler and trading schooner, and is a favourite fishing-ground of the people of Nanomaga--when the sharks give them a chance.

\* \* \* \*

One night Atupa, Chief of Nanomaga, caused a huge fire to be lit on the beach as a signal to the people of Nanomea that a MALAGA, or party of voyagers, was coming over. Both islands are low--not more than fifteen feet above sea-level--and are distant from one another about thirty-eight miles. The following night the reflection of the answering fire on Nanomea was seen, and Atupa prepared to send away his people in seven canoes. They would start at sundown, so as to avoid paddling in the heat (the Nanomagans have no sailing canoes), and be guided to Nanomea, which they expected to reach early in the morning, by the far distant glare of the great fires of coconut and pandanus leaves kindled at intervals of a few hours. About seventy people were to go, and all that day the little village busied itself in preparing for the Nanomeans gifts of foods--cooked PURAKA, fowls, pigs, and flying-fish.

\* \* \* \*

Atupa, the heathen chief, was troubled in his mind in those days of August 1872. The JOHN WILLIAMS had touched at the island and landed a Samoan missionary, who had pressed him to accept Christianity. Atupa, dreading a disturbing element in his little community, had, at first, declined; but the ship had come again, and the chief having consented to try the new religion, a teacher landed. But since then he and his sub-chiefs had consulted the oracle, and had been told that the shades of Maumau Tahori and Foilagi, their deified ancestors, had answered that the new religion was unacceptable to them, and that the Samoan teacher must be killed or sent away. And for this was Atupa sending off some of his people to Nano-mea with gifts of goodwill to the chiefs to beseech them to consult their oracles also, so that the two islands might take concerted action against this new foreign god, whose priests said that all men were equal, that all were bad, and He and His Son alone good.

\* \* \* \*

The night was calm when the seven canoes set out. Forty men and thirty women and children were in the party, and the craft were too deeply laden for any but the smoothest sea. On the AMA (outrigger) of each canoe were the baskets of food and bundles of mats for their hosts, and seated on these were the children, while the women sat with the men and helped them to paddle. Two hours' quick paddling brought them to the shoal-water of Tia Kau, and at the same moment they saw to the N.W. the sky-glare of the first guiding fire.

\* \* \* \*

It was then that the people in the first canoe, wherein was Palu, the daughter of Atupa, called out to those behind to prepare their ASU (balers), as a heavy squall was coming down from the eastward. Then Laheu, an old warrior in another canoe, cried out that they should return on their track a little and get into deep water; "for," said he, "if we swamp, away from Tia Kau, it is but a little thing, but here--" and he clasped his hands rapidly together and then tore them apart. They knew what he meant--the sharks that, at night-time forsaking the deep waters, patrolled in droves of thousands the shallow waters of the reef to devour the turtle and the schools of TAFAU ULI and other fish. In quick, alarmed silence the people headed back, but even then the first fierce squall struck them, and some of the frail canoes began to fill at once. "I MATAGI! I MATAGI! (head to the wind)" a man called out; "head to the wind, or we perish! 'Tis but a puff and it is gone."

\* \* \* \*

But it was more than a puff. The seven canoes, all abreast, were still in shallow water, and the paddlers kept them dead in the teeth of the whistling wind and stinging rain, and called out words of encouragement to one another and to the women and children, as another black squall burst upon them and the curling seas began to break. The canoe in which was Atupa's daughter was the largest and best of all the seven, but was much overladen, and on the outrigger grating were four children. These the chief's daughter was endeavouring to shield from the rain by covering them with a mat, when one of them, a little girl, endeavoured to steady herself by holding to one of the thin pieces of grating; it broke, and her arm fell through and struck the water, and in an instant she gave a dull, smothered wail. Palu, the woman, seized her by her hair and pulled the child up to a sitting posture, and then shrieked with terror--the girl's arm was gone.

\* \* \* \*

And then in the blackness of night, lightened now by the white, seething, boiling surge, the people saw in the phosphorescent water countless hundreds of the savage terrors of the Tia Kau darting hither and thither amongst the canoes--for the smell of blood had brought them together instantly. Presently a great grey monster tore the paddle from out the hands of the steersman of the canoe wherein were the terrified Palu and the four children, and then, before the man for'ard could bring her head to the wind, she broached to and filled. Like ravening wolves the sharks dashed upon their prey, and ere the people had time to give more than a despairing cry, those hideous jaws and gleaming cruel teeth had sealed their fate. Maddened with fear, the rest of the people threw everything out of the six other canoes to lighten them, and as the bundles of mats and baskets of food touched the water the sharks seized and bit, tore and swallowed. Then, one by one, every paddle was grabbed from the hands of the paddlers, and the canoes broached to and filled in that sea of death--all save one, which was carried by the force of the wind away from the rest. In this were the only survivors--two men.

\* \* \* \*

The agony could not have lasted long. "Were I to live as long as he whom the FAIFEAU (missionary) tells us lived to be nine hundred and sixty and nine, I shall hear the groans and cries and shrieks of that PO MALAIA, that night of evil luck," said one of the two who lived, to Denison, the white trader at Nanomea. "Once did I have my paddle fast in the mouth of a little devil, and it drew me backwards, backwards, over the stern till my head touched the water. TAH! but I was strong with fear, and held on, for to lose it meant death by the teeth. And Tulua--he who came out alive with me, seized my feet and held on, else had I gone. But look thou at this"--and he pointed to his scarred neck and back and shoulders "ere I could free my FOE (paddle) and raise my head, I was bitten thus by others. Ah, PAPALAGI, some men are born to wisdom, but most are fools. Had not Atupa been filled with vain fears, he had killed the man who caused him to lose so many of our people."

"So," said the white man, "and wouldst thou have killed the man who brought thee the new faith? Fie!"

"Aye, that would I--in those days when I was PO ULI ULI [Heathen, lit. "In the blackest night"]. But not now, for I am Christian. Yet had Atupa killed and buried the stranger, we could have lied and said he died of a sickness when they of his people came to seek him. And then had I now my son Tagipo with me, he who went into the bellies of the sharks at Tia Kau."

# PALLOU'S TALOI
## A Memory Of The Paumotus

I stayed once at Rotoava--in the Low Archipelago, Eastern Polynesia--while suffering from injuries received in a boat accident one wild night. My host, the Rotoava trader, was a sociable old pirate, whose convivial soul would never let him drink alone. He was by trade a boat-builder, having had, in his early days, a shed at Miller's Point, in Sydney, where he made money and married a wife. But this latter event was poor Tom Oscott's undoing, and in the end he took his chest of tools on board the THYRA trading brig, and sailed away to Polynesia. Finally, after many years' wandering, he settled down at Rotoava as a trader and boat-builder, and became a noted drinker of bottled beer.

The only method by which I could avoid his incessant invitations to "have another" was to get his wife and children to carry me down to his work-shed, built in a lovely spot surrounded by giant PUKA trees. Here, under the shade, I had my mats spread, and with one of his children sitting at my head to fan away the flies, I lay and watched, through the belt of coconuts that lined the beach, the blue rollers breaking on the reef and the snow-white boatswain-birds floating high overhead.

\* \* \* \*

Tom was in the bush one morning when his family carried me to the boat-shed. He had gone for a log of seasoned TOA wood [A hard wood much used in boat building] to another village. At noon he returned, and I heard him bawling for me. His little daughter, the fly-brusher, gave an answering yell, and then Tom walked down the path, carrying two bottles of beer; behind him Lucia, his eldest daughter, a monstrous creature of giggles, adipose tissue, and warm heart, with glasses and a plate of crackers; lastly, old Marie, the wife, with a little table.

"By ----, you've a lot more sense'n me. It's better lyin' here in the cool, than foolin' around in the sun; so I've brought yer suthin' to drink."

"Oh, Tom," I groaned, "I'm sure that beer's bad for me."

The Maker of Boats sat on his bench, and said that he knew of a brewer's carter in Sydney who, at Merriman's "pub," on Miller's Point, had had a cask of beer roll over him. Smashed seven ribs, one arm, and one thigh. Doctors gave him up; undertaker's man called on his wife for coffin order but a sailor chap said he'd pull him through. Got an indiarubber tube and made him suck up as much beer as he could hold; kept it up till all his bones "setted" again, and he recovered. Why shouldn't I--if I only drank enough?

"Hurry up, old dark-skin!"--this to the faded Marie. Uttering merely the word "Hog!" she drew the cork. I had to drink some, and every hour or so Tom would say it was very hot, and open yet another bottle. At last I escaped the beer by nearly dying, and then the kind old fellow hurried away in his boat to Apatiki--another island of the group--and came back with some bottles of claret, bought from the French trader there. With him came two visitors--a big half-caste of middle age, and his wife, a girl of twenty or there-about. This was Edward Pallou and his wife Taloi.

\* \* \* \*

I was in the house when Tom returned, enjoying a long-denied smoke. Pallou and his wife entered and greeted me. The man was a fine, well-set-up fellow, wiry and muscular, with deep-set eyes, and bearing across his right cheek a heavy scar. His wife was a sweet, dainty little creature with red lips, dazzling teeth, hazel eyes, and long wavy hair. The first thing I noticed about her was, that instead of squatting on a mat in native fashion, she sank into a wide chair, and lying back enquired, with a pleasant smile and in perfect English, whether I was feeling any better. She was very fair, even for a Paumotuan half-caste, as I thought she must be, and I said to Pallou, "Why, any one would take your wife to be an Englishwoman!"

"Not I," said Taloi, with a rippling laugh, as she commenced to make a banana-leaf cigarette; "I am a full-blooded South Sea Islander. I belong to Apatiki, and was born there. Perhaps I have white blood in me. Who knows?--only my wise mother. But when I was twelve years old I was adopted by a gentleman in Papeite, and he sent me to Sydney to school. Do you know Sydney? Well, I was three years with the Misses F----, in ---- Street. My goodness! I WAS glad to leave--and so were the Misses F---- to see me go. They said I was downright wicked, because one day I tore the dress off a girl who said my skin was tallowy, like my name. When I came back to Tahiti my guardian took me to Raiatea, where he had a business, and said I must marry him, the beast!"

"Oh, shut up, Taoi!" growled the deep-voiced Pallou, who sat beside me. "What the deuce does this man care about your doings?"

"Shut up yourself, you brute! Can't I talk to any one I like, you turtle-headed fool? Am I not a good wife to you, you great, over-grown savage? Won't you let a poor devil of a woman talk a little? Look here, Tom, do you see that flash jacket he's wearing? Well, I sat up two nights making that--for him to come over here with, and show off before the Rotoava girls. Go and die, you ----!"

The big half-caste looked at Tom and then at me. His lips twitched with suppressed passion, and a dangerous gleam shone a moment in his dark eyes.

"Here, I say, Taloi," broke in Tom, good-humouredly, "just go easy a bit with Ted. As for him a-looking at any of the girls here, I knows better--and so do you."

Taloi's laugh, clear as the note of a bird, answered him, and then she said she was sorry, and the lines around Pallou's rigid mouth softened down. It was easy to see that this grim half-white loved, for all her bitter tongue, the bright creature who sat in the big chair.

Presently Taloi and Lucia went out to bathe, and Pallou remained with me. Tom joined us, and for a while no one spoke. Then the trader, laying down his pipe on the table, drew his seat closer, and commenced, in low tones, a conversation in Tahitian with Pallou. From the earnest manner of old Tom and the sullen gloom that overspread Pallou's face, I could discern that some anxiety possessed them.

At last Tom addressed me. "Look here, ----, Ted here is in a mess, and we've just been a-talkin' of it over, and he says perhaps you'll do what you can for him."

The half-caste turned his dark eyes on me and looked intently into mine.

"What is it, Tom?"

"Well, you see, it come about this way. You heard this chap's missus--Taloi--a-talkin' about the Frenchman that wanted to marry her. He had chartered a little schooner in Papeite to go to Raiatea. Pallou here was mate, and, o' course, he being from the same part of the group as Taloi, she ups and tells him that the Frenchman wanted to marry her straightaway; and then I s'pose, the two gets a bit chummy, and Pallou tells her that if she didn't want the man he'd see as how she wasn't forced agin' her will. So when the vessel gets to Raiatea it fell calm, just about sunset. The Frenchman was in a hurry to get ashore, and tells his skipper to put two men in the boat and some grub, as he meant to pull ashore to his station. So they put the boat over the side, and Frenchy and Taoi and Pallou and two native chaps gets in and pulls for the land. "They gets inside Uturoa about midnight. 'Jump out,' says the Frenchman to Taloi as soon as the boat touches the beach; but the girl wouldn't, but ties herself up around Pallou and squeals. 'Sakker!' says the Frenchy, and he grabs her by the hair and tries to tear her away. ''Ere, stop that,' says Pallou; 'the girl ain't willin',' an' he pushes Frenchy away. 'Sakker!' again, and Frenchy whips out his pistol and nearly blows Pallou's face off'n him; and then, afore he knows how it was done, Ted sends his knife chunk home into the other fellow's throat. The two native sailors runned away ashore, and Pallou and Taloi takes the oars and pulls out again until they drops. Then a breeze comes along, and they up stick and sails away and gets clear o' the group, and brings up, after a lot of sufferin', at Rurutu. And ever since then there's been a French gunboat a-lookin' for Pallou, and he's been hidin' at Apatiki for nigh on a twelvemonth, and has come over here now to see if, when your ship comes back, you can't give him and his missus a passage away somewhere to the westward, out o' the run of that there gunboat, the VAUDREUIL."

* * * *

I promised I would "work it" with the captain, and Pallou put out his brawny hand--the hand that "drove it home into Frenchy's throat"--and grasped mine in silence. Then he lifted his jacket and showed me his money-belt, filled.

"I don't want money," I said. "If you have told me the whole story, I would help any man in such a fix as you." And then Taloi, fresh from her bath, came in and sat down on the mat, whilst fat Lucia combed and dressed her glossy hair and placed therein scarlet hisbiscus flowers; and to show her returned good temper, she took from her lips the cigarette she was smoking, and offered it to the grim Pallou.

A month later we all three left Rotoava, and Pallou and Taloi went ashore at one of the Hervey Group, where I gave him charge of a station with a small stock of trade, and we sailed away east-ward to Pitcairn and Easter Islands.

\* \* \* \*

Pallou did a good business, and was well liked; and some seven months afterwards, when we were at Maga Reva, in the Gambier Group, I got a letter from him. "Business goes well," he wrote, "but Taloi is ill; I think she will die. You will find everything square, though, when you come."

But I was never to see that particular island again, as the firm sent another vessel in place of ours to get Pallou's produce. When the captain and the supercargo went ashore, a white trader met them, with a roll of papers in his hand.

"Pallou's stock-list," he said.

"Why, where is he? gone away?"

"No, he's here still; planted alongside his missus."

"Dead!"

"Yes. A few months after he arrived here, that pretty little wife of his died. He came to me, and asked if I would come and take stock with him. I said he seemed in a bit of a hurry to start stocktaking before the poor thing was buried; but anyhow, I went, and we took stock, and he counted his cash, and asked me to lock the place up if anything happened to him. Then we had a drink, and he bade me good-day, and said he was going to sit with Taloi awhile, before they took her away. He sent the native women out of the bedroom, and the next minute I heard a shot. He'd done it, right enough. Right through his brain, poor chap. I can tell you he thought a lot of that girl of his. There's the two graves, over there by that FETAU tree. Here's his stock-list and bag of cash and keys. Would you mind giving me that pair of rubber sea-boots he left?"

# A BASKET OF BREAD-FRUIT

It was in Steinberger's time [Colonel Steinberger, who in 1874 succeeded in forming a government in Samoa]. A trader had come up to Apia in his boat from the end of Savaii, the largest of the Samoan Group, and was on his way home again, when the falling tide caused him to stop awhile at Mulinu'u Point, about two miles from Apia. Here he designed to smoke and talk, and drink kava at the great camp with some hospitable native acquaintances, during the rising of the water. Soon he was taking his ease on a soft mat, watching the bevy of AUA LUMA [The local girls] making a bowl of kava.

Now this trader lived at Falealupo, at the extreme westerly end of Savaii; but the Samoans, by reason of its isolation and extremity, have for ages called it by another name--an unprintable one--and so some of the people present began to jest with the trader for living in such a place. He fell in with their humour, and said that if those present would find for him a wife, a girl unseared by the breath of scandal, he would leave Falealupo for Safune, where he had bought land.

"Malie!" said an old dame, with one eye and white hair, "the PAPALAGI [foreigner] is inspired to speak wisdom to-night; for at Safune grow the sweetest nuts and the biggest taro and bread-fruit; and lo! here among the kava-chewers is a young maid from Safune--mine own grand-daughter Salome. And against her name can no one in Samoa laugh in the hollow of his hand," and the old creature, amid laughter and cries of ISA! E LE MA LE LO MATUA (The old woman is without shame), crept over to the trader, and, with one skinny hand on his knee, gazed steadily into his face with her one eye.

* * * *

The trader looked at the girl--at Salome. She had, at her grandmother's speech, turned her head aside, and taking the "chaw" of kava-root from her pretty mouth, dissolved into shame-faced tears. The trader was a man of quick perceptions, and he made up his mind to do in earnest what he had said in jest--this because of the tears of Salome. He quickly whispered to the old woman, "Come to the boat before the full of the tide, and we will talk."

When the kava was ready for drinking the others present had forgotten all about the old woman and Salome, who had both crept away unobserved, and an hour or two was passed in merriment, for the trader was a man well liked. Then, when he rose and said TO FA, [good-bye] they begged him not to attempt to pass down in his boat inside the reef, as he was sure to be fired upon, for how were their people to tell a friend from an enemy in the black night? But the white man smiled, and said his boat was too heavily laden to face the ocean swell. So they bade him TO FA, and called out MANUIA OE! [Bless you!] as he lifted the door of thatch and went.

* * * *

The old woman awaited him, holding the girl by the hand. On the ground lay a basket strongly tied up. Salome still wept, but the old woman angrily bade her cease and enter the boat, which the crew had now pushed bow-on to the beach. The old woman lifted the basket and carefully put it on board.

"Be sure," she said to the crew, "not to sit on it for it is very ripe bread-fruit that I am taking to my people in Manono."

"Give them here to me," said the trader, and he put the basket in the stern out of the way. The old woman came aft, too, and crouched at his feet and smoked a SULUI [a cigarette rolled in dried banana leaf]. The cool land-breeze freshened as the sail was hoisted, and then the crew besought the trader not to run down inside the reef. Bullets, they said, if fired in plenty, always hit something, and the sea was fairly smooth outside the reef. And old Lupetea grasped his hand and muttered in his ear, "For the sake of this my little daughter go outside. See, now, I am old, and to lie when so near death as I am is foolish. Be warned by me and be wise; sail out into the ocean, and at daylight we shall be at Salua in Manono. Then thou canst set my feet on the shore--I and the basket. But the girl shall go with thee. Thou canst marry her, if that be to thy mind, in the fashion of the PAPALAGI, or take her FA'A SAMOA [Samoan fashion]. Thus will I keep faith with thee. If the girl be false, her neck is but little and thy fingers strong."

Now the trader thought in this wise: "This is well for me, for if I get the girl away thus quietly from all her relations I shall save much in presents," and his heart rejoiced, for although not mean he was a careful man. So he steered his boat seaward, between the seething surf that boiled and hissed on both sides of the boat passage.

* * * *

As the boat sailed past the misty line of cloud-capped Upolu, the trader lifted the girl up beside him and spoke to her. She was not afraid of him, she said, for many had told her he was a good man, and not an ULA VALE (scamp), but she wept because now, save her old grandmother, all her kinsfolk were dead. Even but a day and a half ago her one brother was killed with her cousin. They were strong men, but the bullets were swift, and so they died. And their heads had been shown at Matautu. For that she had grieved and wept and eaten nothing, and the world was cold and dark to her.

"Poor little devil!" said the trader to himself--"hungry." Then he opened a locker and found a tin of sardines. Not a scrap of biscuit. There was plenty of biscuit, though, in the boat, in fifty-pound tins, but on these mats were spread, where-on his crew were sleeping. He was about to rouse them when he remembered the old dame's basket of ripe bread-fruit. He laughed and looked at her. She, too, slept, coiled up at his feet. But first he opened the sardines and placed them beside the girl, and motioned her to steer. Her eyes gleamed like diamonds in the darkness as she answered his glance, and her soft fingers grasped the tiller. Very quickly, then, he felt among the packages aft till he came to the basket.

A quick stroke of his knife cut the cinnet that lashed the sides together. He felt inside. "Only two, after all, but big ones, and no mistake. Wrapped in cloth, too! I wonder--Hell and Furies! what's this?"--as his fingers came in contact with something that felt like a human eye. Drawing his hand quickly back, he fumbled in his pockets for a match, and struck it. Bread-fruit! No. Two heads with closed eyes and livid lips blue with the pallor of death, showing their white teeth. And Salome covered her face and slid down in the bottom of the boat again, and wept afresh for her cousin and brother, and the boat came up in the wind, but no one awoke.

* * * *

The trader was angry. But after he had tied up the basket again he put the boat on her course once more and called to the girl. She crept close to him and nestled under his overcoat, for the morning air came across the sea from the dew-laden forests, and she was chilled. Then she told the story of how her granddam had begged the heads from those of Malietoa's troops who had taken them at Matautu, and then gone to the camp at Mulinu'u in the hope of getting a passage in some boat to Manono, her country, where she would fain bury them. And that night he had come, and old Lupetea had rejoiced, and sworn her to secrecy about the heads in the basket. And that also was why Lupetea was afraid of the boat going down inside the passage, for there were many enemies to be met with, and they would have shot old Lupetea because she was of Manono. That was all. Then she ate the sardines, and, leaning her head against the trader's bosom, fell asleep.

* * * *

As the first note of the great grey pigeon sounded the dawn, the trader's boat sailed softly up to the Salua beach, and old Lupetea rose, and, bidding the crew good-bye, and calling down blessings on the head of the good and clever white man, as she rubbed his and the girl's noses against her own, she grasped her Basket of Bread-fruit and went ashore. Then the trader, with Salome nestling to his side, sailed out again into the ocean towards his home.

# ENDERBY'S COURTSHIP

The two ghastly creatures sat facing each other in their wordless misery as the wind died away and the tattered remnants of the sail hung motionless after a last faint flutter. The Thing that sat aft--for surely so grotesquely horrible a vision could not be a Man--pointed with hands like the talons of a bird of prey to the purple outline of the island in the west, and his black, blood-baked lips moved, opened, and essayed to speak. The other being that, with bare and skinny arms clasped around its bony knees, sat crouched in the bottom of the boat, leaned forward to listen.

"Ducie Island, Enderby," said the first in a hoarse, rattling whisper; "no one on it; but water is there . . . and plenty of birds and turtle, and a few coconuts."

At the word "water" the listener gave a curious gibbering chuckle, unclasped his hands from his knees, and crept further towards the speaker.

"And the current is setting us down to it, wind or no wind. I believe we'll see this pleasure-trip through, after all"--and the black lips parted in a hideous grimace.

The man whom he called Enderby sank his head again upon his knees, and his dulled and bloodshot eyes rested on something that lay at the captain's feet--the figure of a woman enveloped from her shoulders down in a ragged native mat. For some hours past she had lain thus, with the grey shadows of coming dissolution hovering about her pallid face, and only the faintest movement of lips and eyelids to show that she still lived.

\* \* \* \*

The black-whiskered man who steered looked down for a second upon the face beneath him with the unconcern for others born of the agony of thirst and despair, and again his gaunt face turned to the land. Yet she was his wife, and not six weeks back he had experienced a cold sort of satisfaction in the possession of so much beauty.

He remembered that day now. Enderby, the passenger from Sydney, and he were walking the poop; his wife was asleep in a deck-chair on the other side. An open book lay in her lap. As the two men passed and re-passed her, the one noted that the other would glance in undisguised and honest admiration at the figure in the chair. And Enderby, who was as open as the day, had said to him, Langton, that the sleeping Mrs Langton made as beautiful a picture as he had ever seen.

\* \* \* \*

The sail stirred, filled out, and then drooped again, and the two spectres, with the sleeping woman between, still sat with their hungry eyes gazing over toward the land. As the sun sank, the outlines of the verdure-clad summits and beetling cliffs stood forth clearly for a short minute or two, as if to mock them with hope, and then became enshrouded in the tenebrous night.

\* \* \* \*

Another hour, and a faint sigh came from the ragged mat. Enderby, for ever on the watch, had first seen a white hand silhouetted against the blackness of the covering, and knew that she was still alive. And as he was about to call Langton, who lay in the stern-sheets muttering in hideous dreams, he heard the woman's voice calling HIM. With panting breath and trembling limbs he crawled over beside her and gently touched her hand.

"Thank God, you are alive, Mrs Langton. Shall I wake Captain Langton? We must be nearing the land."

"No, don't. Let him sleep. But I called you, Mr Enderby, to lift me up. I want to see where the rain is coming from."

Enderby groaned in anguish of spirit. "Rain? God has forgotten us, I ----," and then he stopped in shame at betraying his weakness before a woman.

The soft, tender tones again--"Ah, do help me up, please, I can FEEL the rain is near." Then the man, with hot tears of mingled weakness and pity coursing down his cheeks, raised her up.

"Why, there it is, Mr Enderby--and the land as well! And it's a heavy squall, too," and she pointed to a moving, inky mass that half concealed the black shadow of the island. "Quick, take my mat; one end of it is tight and will hold water."

"Langton, La-a-ngton! Here's a rain squall coming!" and Enderby pressed the woman's hand to his lips and kissed it again and again. Then with eager hands he took the mat from her, and staggering forward to the bows stretched the sound end across and bellied it down. And then the moving mass that was once black, and was now white, swept down upon them, and brought them life and joy.

Langton, with an empty beef-tin in his hand, stumbled over his wife's figure, plunged the vessel into the water and drank again and again.

"Curse you, you brute!" shouted Enderby through the wild noise of the hissing rain, "where is your wife? Are you going to let her lie there without a drink?"

Langton answered not, but drank once more. Then Enderby, with an oath, tore the tin from his hand, filled it and took it to her, holding her up while she drank. And as her eyes looked gratefully into his while he placed her tenderly back in the stern-sheets, the madness of a moment overpowered him, and he kissed her on the lips.

Concerned only with the nectar in the mat, Langton took no regard of Enderby as he opened the little locker, pulled out a coarse dungaree jumper, and wrapped it round the thinly-clad and drenched figure of the woman.

She was weeping now, partly from the joy of knowing that she was not to die of the agonies of thirst in an open boat in mid-Pacific, and partly because the water had given her strength to remember that Langton had cursed her when he had stumbled over her to get at the water in the mat.

* * * *

She had married him because of his handsome face and dashing manner for one reason, and because her pious Scotch father, also a Sydney-Tahitian trading captain, had pointed out to her that Langton had made and was still making money in the island trade. Her ideal of a happy life was to have her husband leave the sea and buy an estate either in Tahiti or Chili. She knew both countries well: the first was her birthplace, and between there and Valparaiso and Sydney her money-grubbing old father had traded for years, always carrying with him his one daughter, whose beauty the old man regarded as a "vara vain thing," but likely to procure him a "weel-to-do mon" for a son-in-law.

Mrs Langton cared for her husband in a prosaic sort of way, but she knew no more of his inner nature and latent utter selfishness a year after her marriage than she had known a year before. Yet, because of the strain of dark blood in her veins--her mother was a Tahitian half-caste--she felt the mastery of his savage resolution in the face of danger in the thirteen days of horror that had elapsed since the brigantine crashed on an uncharted reef between Pitcairn and Ducie Islands, and the other boat had parted company with them, taking most of the provisions and water. And to hard, callous natures such as Langton's women yield easily and admire--which is better, perhaps, than loving, for both.

But that savage curse still sounded in her ears, and unconsciously made her think of Enderby, who had always, ever since the eighth day in the boat, given her half his share of water. Little did she know the agony it cost him the day before when the water had given out, to bring her the whole of his allowance. And as she drank, the man's heart had beaten with a dull sense of pity, the while his baser nature called out, "Fool! it is HIS place, not yours, to suffer for her."

\* \* \* \*

At daylight the boat was close in to the land, and Langton, in his cool, cynical fashion, told his wife and Enderby to finish up the last of the meat and biscuit--for if they capsized getting through into the lagoon, he said, they would never want any more. He had eaten all he wanted unknown to the others, and looked with an unmoved face at Enderby soaking some biscuit in the tin for his wife. Then, with the ragged sail fluttering to the wind, Langton headed the boat through the passage into the glassy waters of the lagoon, and the two tottering men, leading the woman between them, sought the shelter of a thicket scrub, impenetrable to the rays of the sun, and slept. And then for a week Enderby went and scoured the reefs for food for her.

\* \* \* \*

One day at noon Enderby awoke. The woman still slept heavily, the first sign of returning strength showing as a faint tinge in the pallor of her cheek. Langton was gone. A sudden chill passed over him--had Langton taken the boat and left them to die on lonely Ducie? With hasty step Enderby hurried to the beach. The boat was there, safe. And at the farther end of the beach he saw Langton, sitting on the sand, eating.

"Selfish brute!" muttered Enderby. "I wonder what he's got?" just then he saw, close overhead, a huge ripe pandanus, and, picking up a heavy, flat piece of coral, he tried to ascend the triplicated bole of the tree and hammer off some of the fruit. Langton looked up at him, and showed his white teeth in a mocking smile at the futile effort. Enderby walked over to him, stone in hand. He was not a vindictive man, but he had grown to hate Langton fiercely during the past week for his selfish neglect of his wife. And here was the fellow. gorging himself on turtle-eggs, and his tender, delicate wife living on shell-fish and pandanus.

\* \* \* \*

"Langton," he said, speaking thickly and pretending not to notice the remainder of the eggs, "the tide is out, and we may get a turtle in one of the pools if you come with me. Mrs Langton needs something better than that infernal pandanus fruit. Her lips are quite sore and bleeding from eating it."

The Inner Nature came out. "Are they? My wife's lips seem to give you a very great deal of concern. She has not said anything to me. And I have an idea----" the look in Enderby's face shamed into silence the slander he was about to utter. Then he added coolly--"But as for going with you after a turtle, thanks, I won't. I've found a nest here, and have had a good square feed. If the cursed man-o'-war hawks and boobies hadn't been here before me I'd have got the whole lot." Then he tore the skin off another egg with his teeth.

With a curious guttural voice Enderby asked--"How many eggs were left?"

"Thirty or so--perhaps forty."

"And you have eaten all but those?"--pointing with savage contempt to five of the round, white balls; "give me those for your wife."

"My dear man, Louise has too much Island blood in her not to be able to do better than I--or you--in a case like ours. And as you have kindly constituted yourself her providore, you had better go and look for a nest yourself."

"You dog!"--and the sharp-edged coral stone crashed into his brain.

\* \* \* \*

When Enderby returned, he found Mrs Langton sitting up on the creeper-covered mound that over-looked the beach where he had left Langton.

"Come away from here," he said, "into the shade. I have found a few turtle-eggs."

They walked back a little and sat down. But for the wild riot in his brain, Enderby would have noted that every vestige of colour had left her face.

"You must be hungry," he thought he was saying to her, and he placed the white objects in her lap.

She turned them slowly over and over in her hands, and then dropped them with a shudder. Some were flecked with red.

"For God's sake," the man cried, "tell me what you know!"

"I saw it all," she answered.

"I swear to you, Mrs Lan----" (the name stuck in his throat) "I never meant it. As God is my witness, I swear it. If we ever escape from here I will give myself up to justice as a murderer." The woman, with hands spread over her face, shook her head from side to side and sobbed. Then she spoke. "I thought I loved him, once. . . . Yet it was for me . . . and you saved my life over and over again in the boat. All sinners are forgiven we are told. . . . Why should not you be? . . . and it was for me you did it. And I won't let you give yourself up to justice or any one. I'll say he died in the boat." And then the laughter of hysterics.

\* \* \* \*

When, some months later, the JOSEPHINE, whaler, of New London, picked them up on her way to Japan, VIA the Carolines and Pelews, the captain satisfactorily answered the query made by Enderby if he could marry them. He "rayther thought he could. A man who was used ter ketchin' and killin'whales, the powerfullest creature of Almighty Gawd's creation, was ekal to marryin' a pair of unfortunit human beans in sich a pre-carus situation as theirs."

\* \* \* \*

And, by the irony of fate, the Enderbys (that isn't their name) are now living in a group of islands where there's quite a trade done in turtle, and whenever a ship's captain comes to dine with them they never have the local dish--turtle eggs--for dinner. "We see them so often," Enderby explains, "and my wife is quite tired of them."

## LONG CHARLEY'S GOOD LITTLE WIFE

There was the island, only ten miles away, and there it had been for a whole week. Sometimes we had got near enough to see Long Charley's house and the figures of natives walking on the yellow beach; and then the westerly current would set us away to leeward again. But that night a squall came up, and in half an hour we were running down to the land. When the lights on the beach showed up we hove-to until daylight, and then found the surf too heavy to let us land.

\* \* \* \*

We got in close to the reef, and could see that the trader's copra-house was full, for there were also hundreds of bags outside, awaiting our boats. It was clearly worth staying for. The trader, a tall, thin, pyjama-clad man, came down to the water's edge, waved his long arm, and then turned back and sat down on a bag of copra. We went about and passed the village again, and once more the long man came to the water's edge, waved his arm, and retired to his seat.

In the afternoon we saw a native and Charley together among the bags; then the native left him, and, as it was now low tide, the kanaka was able to walk to the edge of the reef, where he signalled to us. Seeing that he meant to swim off, the skipper went in as close as possible, and backed his foreyard. Watching his chance for a lull in the yet fierce breakers, the native slid over the reef and swam out to us as only a Line Islander or a Tokelau man can swim.

"How's Charley?" we asked, when the dark man reached the deck.

"Who? Charley? Oh, he fine, plenty copra. Tapa my bowels are filled with the sea--for one dollar! Here ARIKI VAKA (captain) and you TUHI TUHI (supercargo)," said the native, removing from his perforated and pendulous ear-lobe a little roll of leaf, "take this letter from the mean man that giveth but a dollar for facing such a GALU (surf). Hast plenty tobacco on board, friends of my heart? Apa, the surf! Not a canoe crew could the white man get to face it. Is it good twist tobacco, friends, or the flat cakes? Know that I am a man of Nanomea, not one of these dog-eating people here, and a strong swimmer, else the letter had not come."

The supercargo took the note. It was rolled up in many thicknesses of banana-leaf, which had kept it dry--

"DEAR FRIENDS,--I have Been waiting for you for near 5 months. I am Chock full of Cobberah and Shark Fins one Ton. I am near Starved Out, No Biscit, no Beef, no flour, not Enything to Eat. for god's Saik send me a case of Gin ashore if you Don't mean to Hang on till the sea goes Down or I shall Starve. Not a Woman comes Near me because I am Run out of Traid, so please try also to Send a Peece of Good print, as there are some fine Women here from Nukunau, and I think I can get one for a wife if I am smart. If you Can't take my Cobberah, and mean to Go away, send the Squair face [Square face--Hollands gin], for god's saik, and something for the Woman,--Your obliged Friend, CHARLES."

We parcelled a bottle of gin round with a small coir line, and sent it ashore by the Nanomea man. Charley and a number of natives came to the edge of the reef to lend a hand in landing the bearer of the treasure. Then they all waded back to the beach, headed by the white man in the dirty pyjamas and sodden-looking FALA hat. Reaching his house, he turned his following away, and shut the door.

"I bet a dollar that fellow wouldn't swap billets with the angel Gabriel at this partikler moment," said our profane mate thoughtfully.

\* \* \* \*

We started weighing and shipping the copra next day. After finishing up, the solemn Charley invited the skipper and supercargo to remain ashore till morning. His great trouble, he told us, was that he had not yet secured a wife, "a reg'lar wife, y'know." He had, unluckily, "lost the run" of the last Mrs Charley during his absence at another island of the group, and negotiations with various local young women had been broken off owing to his having run out of trade. In the South Seas, as in the civilised world generally, to get the girl of your heart is usually a mere matter of trade. There were, he told us with a melancholy look, "some fine Nukunau girls here on a visit, but the one I want don't seem to care much about stayin', unless all this new trade fetches her."

"Who is she?" enquired the skipper.

"Tibakwa's daughter."

"Let's have a look at her," said the skipper, a man of kind impulses, who felt sorry at the intermittency of the Long One's connubial relations. The tall, scraggy trader shambled to the door and bawled out: "Tibakwa, Tibakwa, Tibakwa, O!" three times.

The people, singing in the big MONIEP or town-house, stopped their monotonous droning, and the name of Tibakwa, was yelled vociferously through-out the village in true Gilbert Group style. In the Gilberts, if a native in one corner of a house speaks to another in the opposite, he bawls loud enough to be heard a mile off.

\* \* \* \*

Tibakwa (The Shark) was a short, squat fellow, with his broad back and chest scored and seamed with an intricate and inartistic network of cicatrices made by sharks' teeth swords. His hair, straight, coarse, and jet-black, was cut away square from just above his eyebrows to the top of his ears, leaving his fierce countenance in a sort of frame. Each ear-lobe bore a load--one had two or three sticks of tobacco, twined in and about the distended circle of flesh, and the other a clasp-knife and wooden pipe. Stripped to the waist he showed his muscular outlines to perfection, and he sat down unasked in the bold, self-confident, half-defiant manner natural to the Line Islander.

\* \* \* \*

"Where's Tirau?" asked the trader.

"Here," said the man of wounds, pointing outside, and he called out in a voice like the bellow of a bull--"TIRAU O, NAKO MAI! (Come here!)"

Tirau came in timidly, clothed only in an AIRIRI or girdle, and slunk into a far corner.

The melancholy trader and the father pulled her out, and she dumped herself down in the middle of the room with a muttered "E PUAK ACARON; KACARON; TE MALAN! (Bad white man)."

"Fine girl, Charley," said the skipper, digging him in the ribs. "Ought to suit you, eh! Make a good little wife."

Negotiations then began anew. Father willing to part, girl frightened--commenced to cry. The astute Charley brought out some new trade. Tirau's eye here displayed a faint interest. Charley threw her, with the air of a prince, a whole piece of turkey twill, 12 yards--value three dollars, cost about 2s. 3d. Tirau put out a little hand and drew it gingerly toward her. Tibakwa gave us an atrocious wink.

"She's cottoned!" exclaimed Charley.

\* \* \* \*

And thus, without empty and hollow display, were two loving hearts made to beat as one. As a practical proof of the solemnity of the occasion, the bridegroom then and there gave Tirau his bunch of keys, which she carefully tied to a strand of her AIRIRI, and, smoking one of the captain's Manillas, she proceeded to bash out the mosquitoes from the nuptial couch with a fan. We assisted her, an hour afterwards, to hoist the sleeping body of Long Charley therein, and, telling her to bathe his head in the morning with cold water, we rose to go.

"Good-bye, Tirau!" we said.

"TIAKAPO [Good-night]", said the good Little Wife, as she rolled up an empty square gin bottle in one of Charley's shirts for a pillow, and disposed her graceful figure on the matted floor beside his bed, to fight mosquitoes until daylight.

# THE METHODICAL MR BURR OF MADURO

One day Ned Burr, a fellow trader, walked slowly up the path to my station, and with a friendly nod sat down and watched intently as, with native assistance, I set about salting some pork. Ned lived thirty miles from my place, on a little island at the entrance to the lagoon. He was a prosperous man, and only drank under the pressure of the monotony caused by the non-arrival of a ship to buy his produce. He would then close his store, and, aided by a number of friendly male natives, start on a case of gin. But never a woman went into Ned's house, though many visited the store, where Ned bought their produce, paid for it in trade or cash, and sent them off, after treating them on a strictly business basis.

Now, the Marshall Island women much resented this. Since Ned's wife had died, ten years previously, the women, backed by the chiefs, had made most decided, but withal diplomatic, assaults upon his celibacy. The old men of his village had respectfully and repeatedly reminded him that his state of singleness was not a direct slight to themselves as leading men alone. If he refused to marry again he surely would not cast such a reflection upon the personal characters of some two or three hundred young girls as to refuse a few of them the position of honorary wives PRO TEM., or until he found one whom he might think worthy of higher honours. But the slow-thinking, methodical trader only opened a bottle of gin, gave them fair words and a drink all round, and absolutely declined to open any sort of matrimonial negotiations.

\* \* \* \*

"I'm come to hev some talk with you when you've finished saltin'," he said, as he rose and meditatively prodded a junk of meat with his forefinger.

"Right, old man," I said. "I'll come now," and we went into the big room and sat down.

"Air ye game ter come and see me get married?" he asked, looking away past me, through the open door, to where the surf thundered and tumbled on the outer reef.

"Ned," I said solemnly, "I know you don't joke, so you must mean it. Of course I will. I'm sure all of us fellows will be delighted to hear you're going to get some nice little CARAJZ [an unmarried girl] to lighten up that big house of yours over there. Who's the girl, Ned?"

"Le-jennabon."

"Whew!" I said, "why, she's the daughter of the biggest chief on Arhnu. I didn't think any white man could get her, even if he gave her people a boat-load of dollars as a wedding-gift."

"Well, no," said Ned, stroking his beard meditatively, "I suppose I SHOULD feel a bit set up; but two years ago her people said that, because I stood to them in the matter of some rifles when they had trouble with King Jibberick, I could take her. She was rather young then, any way; but I've been over to Arhnu several times, and I've had spies out, and damn me if I ever could hear a whisper agin' her. I'm told for sure that her father and uncles would ha' killed any one that came after her. So I'm a-goin' to take her and chance it."

"Ned," I said, "you know your own affairs and these people better than I do. Yet are you really going to pin your faith on a Marshall Island girl? You are not like any of us traders. You see, we know what to expect sometimes, and our morals are a lot worse than those of the natives. And it doesn't harrow our feelings much if any one of us has to divorce a wife and get another; it only means a lot of new dresses and some guzzling, drinking, and speechifying, and some bother in teaching the new wife how to make bread. But your wife that died was a Manhikian--another kind.

They don't breed that sort here in the Marshalls. Think of it twice, Ned, before you marry her."

\* \* \* \*

The girl was a beauty. There are many like her in that far-away cluster of coral atolls. That she was a chief's child it was easy to see; the abject manner in which the commoner natives always behaved themselves in her presence showed their respect for Le-jennabon. Of course we all got very jolly. There were half a dozen of us traders there, and we were, for a wonder, all on friendly terms. Le-jennabon sat on a fine mat in the big room, and in a sweetly dignified manner received the wedding-gifts. One of our number, Charlie de Buis, though in a state of chronic poverty, induced by steadfast adherence to square gin at five dollars a case, made his offerings--a gold locket covering a woman's miniature, a heavy gold ring, and a pair of fat, cross-bred Muscovy ducks. The bride accepted them with a smile.

"Who is this?" she asked, looking at the portrait--"your white wife?" "No," replied the bashful Charles, "another man's. That's why I give it away, curse her! But the ducks I bred myself on Madurocaron;."

\* \* \* \*

A month or two passed. Then, on one Sunday afternoon, about dusk, I saw Ned's whale-boat coming over across the lagoon. I met him on the beach. Trouble was in his face, yet his hard, impassive features were such that only those who knew him well could discover it. Instead of entering the house, he silently motioned me to come further along the sand, where we reached an open spot clear of coco palms. Ned sat down and filled his pipe. I waited patiently. The wind had died away, and the soft swish and swirl of the tide as the ripples lapped the beach was the only sound that broke upon the silence of the night.

\* \* \* \*

"You were right. But it doesn't matter now . . ." He laughed softly. "A week
ago a canoe-party arrived from Ebon. There were two chiefs. Of course they came
to my house to trade. They had plenty of money. There were about a hundred natives belonging to them. The younger man was chief of Likieb--a flash buck. The
first day he saw Le-jennabon he had a lot too much to say to her. I watched him.
Next morning my toddy-cutter came and told me that the flash young chief from
Likieb had stuck him up and drank my toddy, and had said something about my
wife--you know how they talk in parables when they mean mischief. I would have
shot him for the toddy racket, but I was waitin' for a better reason. . . . The old hag
who bosses my cook-shed said to me as she passed, 'Go and listen to a song of cunning over there'--pointing to a clump of bread-fruit trees. I walked over--quietly.
Le-jennabon and her girls were sitting down on mats. Outside the fence was a lad
singing this--in a low voice--

"'Marriage hides the tricks of lovers.'

"Le-jennabon and the girls bent their heads and said nothing. Then the devil's
imp commenced again--

"'Marriage hides the tricks of lovers.'

"Some of the girls laughed and whispered to Le-jennabon. She shook her head,
and looked around timorously. Plain enough, wasn't it? Presently the boy creeps up
to the fence, and drops over a wreath of yellow blossoms. The girls laughed. One of
them picked it up, and offered it to Le-jennabon. She waved it away. Then, again,
the cub outside sang softly--

"'Marriage hides the tricks of lovers,'

"and they all laughed again, and Le-jennabon put the wreath on her head, and
I saw the brown hide of the boy disappear among the trees."

* * * *

I went back to the house. I wanted to make certain she would follow the boy first. After a few minutes some of Le-jennabon's women came to me, and said they were going to the weather side of the island--it's narrer across, as you know--to pick flowers. I said all right, to go, as I was going to do something else, so couldn't come with them. Then I went to the trade-room and got what I wanted. The old cook-hag showed me the way they had gone, and grinned when she saw what I had slid down inside my pyjamas. I cut round and got to the place. I had a right good idea where it was.

* * * *

"The girls soon came along the path, and then stopped and talked to Le-jenna-bon and pointed to a clump of bread-fruit trees standing in an arrow-root patch. She seemed frightened--but went. Half-way through she stopped, and then I saw my beauty raise his head from the ground and march over to her. I jest giv' him time ter enjoy a smile, and then I stepped out and toppled him over. Right through his carcase--them Sharp's rifle make a hole you could put your fist into.

"The girl dropped too--sheer funk. Old Lebauro, the cook, slid through the trees and stood over him, and said, 'U, GUK! He's a fine-made man,' and gave me her knife; and then I collared Le-jennabon, and ----"

"For God's sake, Ned, don't tell me you killed her too!"

He shook his head slowly.

"No, I couldn't hurt HER. But I held her with one hand, she feeling dead and cold, like a wet deck-swab; then the old cook-woman undid my flash man's long hair, and, twining her skinny old claws in it, pulled it taut, while I sawed at the chap's neck with my right hand. The knife was heavy and sharp, and I soon got the job through. Then I gave the thing to Le-jennabon to carry.

\* \* \* \*

"I made her walk in front of me. Every time she dropped the head I slewed her round and made her lift it up again. And the old cook-devil trotted astern o' us. When we came close to the town, I says to Le-jennabon:

"'Do you want to live?'

"'Yes,' says she, in a voice like a whisper.

"'Then sing,' says I, 'sing loud--

"'Marriage hides the tricks of lovers,'

And she sang it in a choky kind of quaver.

"There was a great rush o' people ter see the procession. They stood in a line on both sides of the path, and stared and said nothin'.

"Presently we comes to where all the Likieb chief's people was quartered. They knew the head and ran back for their rifles, but my crowd in the village was too strong, and, o' course, sided with me, and took away their guns. Then the crowd gathers round my place, and I makes Le-jennabon hold up the head and sing again--sing that devil's chant.

"'Listen,' I says to the people, 'listen to my wife singing a love song.' Then I takes the thing, wet and bloody, and slings it into the middle of the Likieb people, and gave Le-jennabon a shove and sent her inside."

\* \* \* \*

I was thinking what would be the best thing to say, and could only manage "It's a bad business, Ned."

"Bad! That's where you're wrong," and, rising, Ned brushed the sand off the legs of his pyjamas. "It's just about the luckiest thing as could ha' happened. Ye see, it's given Le-jennabon a good idea of what may happen to her if she ain't mighty correct. An' it's riz me a lot in the esteem of the people generally as a man who hez business principles."

## A TRULY GREAT MAN
## A Mid-Pacific Sketch

Then the flag of "Bobby" Towns, of Sydney, was still mighty in the South Seas. The days had not come in which steamers with brass-bound super-cargoes, carrying tin boxes and taking orders like merchants' bagmen, for goods "to arrive," exploited the Ellice, Kingsmill, and Gilbert Groups. Bluff-bowed old wave-punchers like the SPEC, the LADY ALICIA and the E. K. BATESON plunged their clumsy hulls into the rolling swell of the mid-Pacific, carrying their "trade" of knives, axes, guns, bad rum, and good tobacco, instead of, as now, white umbrellas, paper boots and shoes, German sewing-machines and fancy prints--"zephyrs," the smartly-dressed paper-collared supercargo of to-day calls them, as he submits a card of patterns to Emilia, the native teacher's wife, who, as the greatest Lady in the Land, must have first choice.

* * * *

In those days the sleek native missionary was an unknown quantity in the Tokelaus and Kingsmills, and the local white trader answered all requirements. He was generally a rough character--a runaway from some Australian or American whaler, or a wandering Ishmael, who, for reasons of his own, preferred living among the intractable, bawling, and poverty-stricken people of the equatorial Pacific to dreaming away his days in the monotonously happy valleys of the Society and Marquesas Groups.

\* \* \* \*

Such a man was Probyn, who dwelt on one of the low atolls of the Ellice Islands. He had landed there one day from a Sydney sperm whaler with a chest of clothes, a musket or two, and a tierce of twist tobacco; with him came a savage-eyed, fierce-looking native wife, over whose bared shoulders and bosom fell long waves of black hair; with her was a child about five years old.

The second mate of the whaler, who was in charge of the boat, not liking the looks of the excited natives who swarmed around the newcomer, bade him a hurried farewell, and pushed away to the ship, which lay-to off the passage with her fore-yard aback. Then the clamorous people pressed more closely around Probyn and his wife, and assailed them with questions.

So far neither of them had spoken. Probyn, a tall, wiry, scanty-haired man, with quiet, deep-set eyes, was standing with one foot on the tierce of tobacco and his hands in his pockets. His wife glared defiantly at some two or three score of reddish-brown women who crowded eagerly around her to stare into her face; holding to the sleeve of her dress was the child, paralysed into the silence of fright.

\* \* \* \*

The deafening babble and frantic gesticulations were perfectly explicable to Probyn, and he apprehended no danger. The head man of the village had not yet appeared, and until he came this wild license of behaviour would continue. At last the natives became silent and parted to the right and left as Tahori, the head man, his fat body shining with coconut oil, and carrying an ebony-wood club in his hand, stood in front of the white man and eyed him up and down. The scrutiny seemed satisfactory. He stretched out his huge, naked arm, and shook Probyn's hand, uttering his one word of Samoan--"TALOFA!" [Lit., "My love to you", the Samoan salutation] and then, in his own dialect, he asked: "What is your name, and what do you want?"

"Sam," replied Probyn. And then, in the Tokelau language, which the wild-eyed people around him fairly understood, "I have come here to live with you and trade for oil"--and he pointed to the tierce of tobacco.

"Where are you from?"

"From the land called Nukunono, in the Tokelau."

"Why come here?"

"Because I killed an enemy there."

"Good!" grunted the fat man; "there are no twists in thy tongue; but why did the boat hasten away so quickly?"

"They were frightened because of the noise. He with the face like a fowl's talked too much"--and he pointed to a long, hatchet-visaged native, who had been especially turbulent and vociferous.

\* \* \* \*

"Ha!" and the fat, bearded face of Tahori turned from the white man to him of whom the white man had spoken--"is it thee, Makoi? And so thou madest the strangers hasten away! That was wrong. Only for thee I had gone to the ship and gotten many things. Come hither!"

Then he stooped and picked up one of Probyn's muskets, handed it to the white man, and silently indicated the tall native with a nod. The other natives fell back. Niabong, Probyn's wife, set her boy on his feet, put her hand in her bosom and drew out a key, with which she opened the chest. She threw back the lid, fixed her black eyes on Probyn, and waited.

Probyn, holding the musket in his left hand, mused a moment. Then he asked:

"Whose man is he?"

"Mine," said Tahori; "he is from Oaitupu, and my bondman."

"Hath he a wife?"

"Nay; he is poor, and works in my PURAKA [A coarse species of taro (ARUM ESCULENTUM) growing on the low-lying atolls of the mid-Pacific.] field!"

"Good," said Probyn, and he motioned to his wife. She dived her hand into the chest and handed him a tin of powder, then a bullet, a cap, and some scraps of paper.

Slowly he loaded the musket, and Tahori, seizing the bondman by his arm, led him out to the open, and stood by, club in hand, on the alert.

Probyn knew his reputation depended on the shot. He raised his musket and fired. The ball passed through the chest of Makoi. Then four men picked up the body and carried it into a house.

\* \* \* \*

Probyn laid down the musket and motioned again to Niabong. She handed him a hatchet and blunt chisel. Tahori smiled pleasantly, and, drawing the little boy to him, patted his head.

Then, at a sign from him, a woman brought Niabong a shell of sweet toddy. The chief sat cross-legged and watched Probyn opening the tierce of tobacco. Niabong locked the box again and sat upon it.

"Who are you?" said Tahori, still caressing the boy, to the white man's wife.

"Niabong. But my tongue twists with your talk here. I am of Naura (Pleasant Island). By-and-by I shall understand it."

"True. He is a great man, thy man," said the chief, nodding at Probyn.

"A great man, truly. There is not one thing in the world but he can do it."

"E MOE [true]," said the fat man, approvingly; "I can see it. Look you, he shall be as my brother, and thy child here shall eat of the best in the land."

Probyn came over with his two hands filled with sticks of tobacco.

"Bring a basket," he said.

A young native girl slid out from the coconut grove at Tahori's bidding, and stood behind him holding a basket. Probyn counted out into it two hundred sticks of tobacco.

"See, Tahori. I am a just man to thee because thou art a just man to me. Here is the price of him that thou gavest to me."

Tahori rose and beckoned to the people to return. "Look at this man. He is a truly great man. His heart groweth from his loins upwards to his throat. Bring food to my house quickly, that he and his wife and child may eat. And to-morrow shall every man cut wood for his house, a house that shall be in length six fathoms, and four in width. Such men as he come from the gods."

# THE DOCTOR'S WIFE

Consanguinity--From A Polynesian Standpoint

Oho!" said Lagisiva, the widow, tossing her hair back over her shoulders, as she raised the heavy, fluted tappa mallet in her thick, strong right hand, and dealt the rough cloth a series of quick strokes--"Oho!" said the dark-faced Lagisiva, looking up at the White Man, "because I be a woman dost think me a fool? I tell thee I know some of the customs of the PAPAL-AGI (the white foreigners). Much wisdom have ye in many things; but again I tell thee, O friend of my sons, that in some other things the people of thy nation--ay, of all white nations, they be as the beasts of the forest--the wild goat and pig--without reason and without shame. TAH! Has not my eldest son, Tui Fau, whom the white men call Bob, lived for seven years in Sini (Sydney), when he returned from those places by New Guinea, where he was diver? And he has filled my ears with the bad and shameless customs of the PAPALAGI. ISA! I say again thy women have not the shame of ours. The heat of desire devoureth chastity even in those of one blood!"

"In what do they offend, O my mother?"

"AUE! Life is short; and, behold, this piece of SIAPO [The tappa cloth of the South Seas, made from the bark of the paper mulberry.] is for a wedding present, and I must hurry; but yet put down thy gun and bag, and we shall smoke awhile, and thou shalt feel shame while I tell of one of the PAPALAGI customs--the mar-rying of brother and sister!"

"Nay, mother," said the White Man, "not brother and sister, but only cous-ins."

"ISA! [an expression of contempt]" and the big widow spat scornfully on the ground, "those are words--words. It is the same; the same is the blood, the same is the bone. Even in our heathen days we pointed the finger at one who looked with the eye of love on the daughter of his father's brother or sister--for such did we let his blood out upon the sand. And I, old Lagisiva, have seen a white man brought to shame through this wickedness!"

"Tell me," said the White Man.

\* \* \* \*

"He was a FOMA'I (doctor), and rich, and came here because he desired to see strange places, and was weary of his life in the land of the PAPALAGI. So he remained with us, and hunted the wild boar with our young men, and became strong and hardy, and like unto one of our people. And then, because he was for ever restless, he sailed away once and returned in a small ship, and brought back trade and built a store and a fine house to dwell in. The chief of this town gave him, for friendship, a piece of land over there by the Vai-ta-milo, and thus did he become a still greater man. His store was full of rich goods, and he kept many servants, and at night-time his house was as a blaze of fire, for the young men and women would go there and sing and dance, and he had many lovers amongst our young girls.

"I, old Lagisiva, who am now fat and dull, was one. Oho, he was a man of plenty! Did a girl but look out between her eyelashes at a piece of print in the store, lo! it was hers, even though it measured twenty fathoms in length--and print was a dollar a fathom in those days. So every girl--even those from parts far off--cast herself in his way, that he might notice her. And he was generous to all alike--in that alone was wisdom.

\* \* \* \*

"Once or twice every year the ships brought him letters. And he would count the marks on the paper, and tell us that they came from a woman of the PAPALA-GI--his cousin, as you would call her--whose picture was hung over his table. She was for ever smiling down upon us, and her eyes were his eyes, and if he but smiled then were the two alike--alike as are two children of the same birth. When three years had come and gone a ship brought him a letter, and that night there were many of us at his house, men and women, to talk with the people from the ship. When those had gone away to their sleep, he called to the chief, and said:--

"'In two days, O my friend, I set out for my land again; but to return, for much do I desire to remain with you always. In six months I shall be here again. And there is one thing I would speak of. I shall bring back a white wife, a woman of my own country, whom I have loved for many years.'

"Then Tamaali'i, the chief, who was my father's father, and very old, said, 'She shall be my daughter, and welcome,' and many of us young girls said also, 'She shall be welcome'--although we felt sorrowful to lose a lover so good and open-handed. And then did the FOMA'I call to the old chief and two others, and they entered the store and lighted lamps, and presently a man went forth into the village, and cried aloud: 'Come hither, all people, and listen!' So, many hundreds came, and we all went in and found the floor covered with some of everything that the white man possessed. And the chief spoke and said:

"'Behold, my people, this our good friend goeth away to his own country that he may bring back a wife. And because many young unmarried girls will say, "Why does he leave us? Are not we as good to look upon as this other woman?" does he put these presents here on the ground and these words into my mouth--"Out of his love to you, which must be a thing that is past and forgotten, the wife that is coming must not know of some little things--that is PAPALAGI custom."'

"And then every girl that had a wish took whatever she fancied, and the white man charged us to say naught that would arouse the anger of the wife that was to come. And so he departed.

\* \* \* \*

"One hundred and ten fat hogs killed we and roasted whole for the feast of welcome. I swear it by the Holy Ones of God's Kingdom--one hundred and ten. And yet this white lily of his never smiled--not even on us young girls who danced and sang before her, only she clung to his arm, and, behold, when we drew close to her we saw it was the woman in the picture--his sister!

"And then one by one all those that had gathered to do him honour went away in shame--shame that he should do this, wed his own sister, and many women said worse of her. But yet the feast--the hogs, and yams, and taro, and fish, and fowls-- was brought and placed by his doorstep, but no one spake, and at night-time he was alone with his wife, till he sent for the old chief, and reproached him with bitter words for the coldness of the people, and asked: 'Why is this?'

\* \* \* \*

"And the old man pointed to the picture over the table, and said: 'Is this she-- thy wife?'

"'Ay,' said the White Man.

"'Is she not of the same blood as thyself?'

"'Even so,' said he.

"'Then shalt thou live alone in thy shame,' said the old man; and he went away.

"So, for many months, these two lived. He found some to work for him, and some young girls to tend his sister, whom he called his wife, whilst she lay ill with her first child. And the day after it was born, some one whispered: 'He is accursed! the child cries not--it is dumb.' For a week it lived, yet never did it cry, for the curse of wickedness was upon it. Then the white man nursed her tenderly, and took her away to live in Fiji for six months. When they came back it was the same--no one cared to go inside his house, and he cursed us, and said he would bring men from Tokelau to work for him. We said naught. Then in time another child was born, and it was hideous to look upon, and that also died.

\* \* \* \*

"Now, there was a girl amongst us whose name was Suni, to whom the white woman spoke much, for she was learning our tongue, and Suni, by reason of the white woman's many presents, spoke openly to her, and told her of the village talk. Then the white woman wept, and arose and spoke to the man for a long while. And she came back to Suni, and said: 'What thou hast told me was in my own heart three years ago; yet, because it is the custom of my people, I married this man, who is the son of my father's brother. But now I shall go away.' Then the white man came out and beat Suni with a stick. But yet was his sister, whom he called his wife, eaten up with shame, and when a ship came they went away, and we saw her not again. For about two years we heard no more of our white man, till he returned and said the woman was dead. And he took Suni for wife, who bore him three children, and then they went away to some other country--I know not where.

\* \* \* \*

"I thank thee many, many times, O friend of my sons. Four children of mine here live in this village, yet not a one of them ever asketh me when I last smoked. May God walk with thee always for this stick of tobacco."

# THE FATE OF THE ALIDA

Three years ago, in an Australian paper, I read something that set me thinking of Taplin--of Taplin and his wife, and the fate of the ALIDA. This is what I read:--

"News has reached Tahiti that a steamer had arrived at Toulon with two noted prisoners on board. These men, who are brothers named Rorique, long ago left Tahiti on an island-trading trip, and when the vessel got to sea they murdered the captain, a passenger, the supercargo (Mr Gibson, of Sydney), and two sailors, and threw their bodies overboard. The movers in the affair were arrested at Ponape, in the Caroline Islands. The vessel belonged to a Tahitian prince, and was called the NUROAHITI, but its name had been changed after the tragedy. The accused persons were sent to Manilla. From Manilla they appear now to have been sent on to France."

[NOTE BY THE AUTHOR.--The brothers Rorique were sentenced to imprisonment for life at Brest in 1895.]

In the year 1872 we were lying inside Funafuti Lagoon, in the Ellice Group. The last cask of oil had been towed off to the brig and placed under hatches, and we were to sail in the morning for our usual cruise among the Gilbert and Kingsmill Islands.

Our captain, a white trader from the shore, and myself, were sitting on deck "yarning" and smoking. We lay about a quarter of a mile from the beach--such a beach, white as the driven snow, and sweeping in a great curve for five long miles to the north and a lesser distance to the south and west. Right abreast of the brig, nestling like huge birds' nests in the shade of groves of coconut and bread-fruit trees, were the houses of the principal village in Funafuti.

Presently the skipper picked up his glasses that lay beside him on the skylight, and looked away down to leeward, where the white sails of a schooner beating up to the anchorage were outlined against the line of palms that fringed the beach of Funafala--the westernmost island that forms one of the chain enclosing Funafuti Lagoon.

"It's Taplin's schooner, right enough," he said. "Let us go ashore and give him and his pretty wife a hand to pack up."

* * * *

Taplin was the name of the only other white trader on Funafuti besides old Tom Humphreys, our own man. He had been two years on the island, and was trading in opposition to our trader, as agent for a foreign house--our owners were Sydney people--but his firm's unscrupulous method of doing business had disgusted him. So one day he told the supercargo of their vessel that he would trade for them no longer than the exact time he had agreed upon--two years. He had come to Funafuti from the Pelews, and was now awaiting the return of his firm's vessel to take him back there again. Getting into our boat we were pulled ashore and landed on the beach in front of the trader's house.

"Well, Taplin, here's your schooner at last," said old Tom, as we shook hands and seated ourselves in the comfortable, pleasant-looking room. "I see you're getting ready to go."

Taplin was a man of about thirty or so, with a quiet, impassive face, and dark, deep-set eyes that gave to his features a somewhat gloomy look, except when he smiled, which was not often. Men with that curious, far-off look in their eyes are not uncommon among the lonely islands of the wide Pacific. Sometimes it comes to a man with long, long years of wandering to and fro; and you will see it deepen when, by some idle, chance word, you move the memories of a forgotten past--ere he had even dreamed of the existence of the South Sea Islands and for ever dissevered himself from all links and associations of the outside world.

\* \* \* \*

"Yes," he answered, "I am nearly ready. I saw the schooner at daylight, and knew it was the ALIDA."

"Where do you think of going to, Taplin?" I asked.

"Back to the Carolines. Nerida belongs down that way, you know; and she is fretting to get back again--otherwise I wouldn't leave this island. I've done pretty well here, although the people I trade for are--well, you know what they are."

"Aye," assented old Humphreys, "there isn't one of 'em but what is the two ends and bight of a--scoundrel; and that supercargo with the yaller moustache and womany hands is the worst of the lot. I wonder if he's aboard this trip? I don't let him inside my house; I've got too many daughters, and they all think him a fine man."

\* \* \* \*

Nerida, Taplin's wife, came out to us from an inner room. She was a native of one of the Pelew Islands, a tall, slenderly-built girl, with pale, olive skin and big, soft eyes. A flowing gown of yellow muslin--the favourite colour of the Portuguese-blooded natives of the Pelews--buttoned high up to her throat, draped her graceful figure. After putting her little hand in ours, and greeting us in the Funafuti dialect, she went over to Taplin, and touching his arm, pointed out the schooner that was now only a mile or so away, and a smile parted her lips, and the star-like eyes glowed and filled with a tender light.

I felt Captain Warren touch my arm as he rose and went outside. I followed.

\* \* \* \*

"L----," said Warren, "can't we do something for Taplin ourselves? Isn't there a station anywhere about Tonga or Wallis Island that would suit him?"

"Would he come, Warren? He--or, rather, that pretty wife of his--seems bent upon going away in the schooner to the Carolines."

"Aye," said the skipper, "that's it. If it were any other vessel I wouldn't care." Then suddenly:

"That fellow Motley (the supercargo) is a damned scoundrel--capable of any villainy where a woman is concerned. Did you ever hear about old Raymond's daughter down at Mangareva?"

I had heard the story very often. By means of a forged letter purporting to have been written by her father--an old English trader in the Gambier Group--Motley had lured the beautiful young half-blood away from a school in San Francisco, and six months afterwards turned her adrift on the streets of Honolulu. Raymond was a lonely man, and passionately attached to his only child; so no one wondered when, reaching California a year after and finding her gone, he shot himself in his room at an hotel.

\* \* \* \*

"I will ask him, anyway," I said; and as we went back into the house the ALI-DA shot past our line of vision through the coco-palms, and brought up inside the brig.

"Taplin," I said, "would you care about taking one of our stations to the eastward? Name any island you fancy, and we will land you there with the pick of our 'trade' room."

"Thank you. I would be only too glad, but I cannot. I have promised Nerida to go back to Babelthouap, or somewhere in the Pelews, and Motley has promised to land us at Ponape, in the Carolines. We can get away from there in one of the Dutch firm's vessels."

"I am very sorry, Taplin----" I began, when old Captain Warren burst in with--"Look here, Taplin, we haven't got much time to talk. Here's the ALIDA'S boat coming, with that (blank blank) scoundrel Motley in it. Take my advice. Don't go away in the ALIDA." And then he looked at Nerida, and whispered something.

A red spark shone in Taplin's dark eyes, then he pressed Warren's hand.

"I know," he answered, "he's a most infernal villain--Nerida hates him too. But you see how I am fixed. The ALIDA is our only chance of getting back to the north-west. But he hasn't got old Raymond to deal with in me. Here they are."

* * * *

Motley came in first, hat and fan in hand. He was a fine-looking man, with blue eyes and an unusually fair skin for an island supercargo, with a long, drooping, yellow moustache. Riedermann, the skipper, who followed, was stout, coarse, red-faced, and brutal.

"How are you, gentlemen?" said Motley affably, turning from Taplin and his wife, and advancing towards us. "Captain Riedermann and I saw the spars of your brig showing up over the coconuts yesterday, and therefore knew we should have the pleasure of meeting you."

Warren looked steadily at him for a moment, and then glanced at his out-stretched hand.

"The pleasure isn't mutual, blarst you, Mr Motley," he said coldly, and he put his hand in his pocket.

The supercargo took a step nearer to him with a savage glare in his blue eyes. "What do you mean by this, Captain Warren?"

"Mean?" and the imperturbable Warren seated himself on a corner of the table, and gazed stolidly first at the handsome Motley and then at the heavy, vicious features of Riedermann. "Oh, anything you like. Perhaps it's because it's not pleasant to see white men landing at a quiet island like this with revolvers slung to their waists under their pyjamas; looks a bit too much like Bully Hayes' style for me," and then his tone of cool banter suddenly changed to that of studied insolence. "I say, Motley, I was talking about you just now to Taplin AND Nerida. Do you want to know what I was saying? Perhaps I had better tell you. I was talking about Tita Raymond--and yourself."

\* \* \* \*

Motley put his right hand under his pyjama jacket, but Taplin sprang forward, seized his wrist in a grip of iron, and drew him aside.

"The man who draws a pistol in my house, Mr Motley, does a foolish thing," he said, in quiet, contemptuous tones, as he threw the supercargo's revolver into a corner.

With set teeth and clenched hands Motley flung himself into a chair, unable to speak.

Warren, still seated on the table, swung his foot nonchalantly to and fro, and then began at Riedermann.

"Why, how's this, Captain Ricdermann? Don't you back up your supercargo's little quarrels, or have you left your pistol on board? Ah, no, you haven't. I can see it there right enough. Modesty forbids you putting a bullet into a man in the presence of a lady, eh?" Then slewing round again, he addressed Motley: "By God! sir, it is well for you that we are in a white man's house, and that that man is my friend and took away that pistol from your treacherous hand. If you had fired at me I would have booted you from one end of Funafuti beach to the other--and I've a damned good mind to do it now, but won't, as Taplin has to do some business with you."

"That will do, Warren," I said. "We don't want to make a scene in Taplin's house. Let us go away and allow him to finish his business."

Still glaring angrily at Riedermann and Motley, Warren got down slowly from the table. Then we bade Taplin and Nerida good-bye and went aboard.

At daylight we saw Taplin and his wife go off in the ALIDA'S boat. They waved their hands to us in farewell as the boat pulled past the brig, and then the schooner hove-up anchor, and with all sail set, stood away down to the north-west passage of the lagoon.

A year or so afterward we were on a trading voyage to the islands of the Tubuai

Group, and were lying becalmed, in company with a New Bedford whaler. Her skipper came on board the brig, and we started talking of Taplin, whom the whale-ship captain knew.

"Didn't you hear?" he said. "The ALIDA never showed up again. 'Turned turtle,' I suppose, somewhere in the islands, like all those slashing, over-masted, 'Frisco-built schooners do, sooner or later."

"Poor Taplin," said Warren, "I thought somehow we would never see him again."

\* \* \* \*

Five years had passed. Honest old Warren, fiery-tempered and true-hearted, had long since died of fever in the Solomons, and I was supercargo with a smart young American skipper in the brigantine PALESTINE, when we one day sailed along the weather-side of a tiny little atoll in the Caroline Islands.

The PALESTINE was leaking, and Packenham, tempted by the easy passage into the beautiful lagoon, decided to run inside and discharge our cargo of copra to get at the leak.

The island had but very few inhabitants--perhaps ten or twelve men and double that number of women and children. No ship, they told us, had ever entered the lagoon but Bully Hayes' brig, and that was nine years before. There was nothing on the island to tempt a trading vessel, and even the sperm whalers, as they lumbered lazily past from Strong's Island to Guam, would not bother to lower a boat and "dicker" for pearl-shell or turtle.

At the time of Hayes' visit the people were in sore straits, and on the brink of actual starvation, for although there were fish and turtle in plenty, they had not the strength to catch them. A few months before, a cyclone had destroyed nearly all the coconut trees, and an epidemic followed it, and carried off half the scanty population.

* * * *

The jaunty sea-rover--than whom a kinder-hearted man to NATIVES never sailed the South Seas--took pity on the survivors, especially the youngest and prettiest girls, and gave them a passage in the famous LEONORA to another island where food was plentiful. There they remained for some years, till the inevitable MAL DU PAYS that is inborn to every Polynesian and Micronesian, became too strong to be resisted; and so one day a wandering sperm whaler brought them back again.

But in their absence strangers had come to the island. As the people landed from the boats of the whale-ship, two brown men, a woman, and a child, came out of one of the houses, and gazed at them. Then they fled to the farthest end of the island and hid.

Some weeks passed before the returned islanders found out the retreat of the strangers, who were armed with rifles, and called them to "come out and be friends." They did so, and by some subtle treachery the two men were killed during the night.

The woman, who was young and handsome, was spared, and, from what we could learn, had been well treated ever since.

"Where did the strangers come from?" we asked.

That they could not tell us. But the woman had since told them that the ship had anchored in the lagoon because she was leaking badly, and that the captain and crew were trying to stop the leak when she began to heel over, and they had barely time to save a few things when she sank. In a few days the captain and crew left the island in the boat, and, rather than face the dangers of a long voyage in such a small boat, the two natives and the woman elected to remain on the island.

"That's a mighty fishy yarn," said Packenham to me. "I daresay these fellows have been doing a little cutting-off business. But then I don't know of any missing vessel. We'll go ashore to-morrow and have a look round."

A little after sunset the skipper and I were leaning over the rail, watching the figures of the natives, as they moved to and fro in the glare of the fires lighted here and there along the beach.

"Hallo!" said Packenham, "here's a canoe coming, with only a woman in it. By thunder! she's travelling, too, and coming straight for the ship."

A few minutes more and the canoe was alongside. The woman hastily picked up a little girl that was sitting in the bottom, looked up, and called out in English--

"Take my little girl, please."

A native sailor leant over the bulwarks and lifted up the child, and the woman clambered after her. Then, seizing the child from the sailor, she flew along the deck and into the cabin.

She was standing facing us as we followed and entered, holding the child tightly to her bosom. The soft light of the cabin lamp fell full upon her features, and we saw that she was very young, and seemed wildly excited.

"Who are you?" we said, when she advanced, put out a trembling hand to us, and said: "Don't you know me, Mr Supercargo? I am Nerida, Taplin's wife." Then she sank on a seat and sobbed violently.

* * * *

We waited till she regained her composure somewhat, and then I said: "Nerida, where is Taplin?"

"Dead," she said in a voice scarce above a whisper; "only us two are left--I and little Teresa."

Packenham held out his hands to the child. With wondering, timid eyes, she came, and for a moment or two looked doubtingly upwards into the brown, handsome face of the skipper, and then nestled beside him.

For a minute or so the ticking of the cabin clock broke the silence, ere I ventured to ask the one question uppermost in my mind.

"Nerida, how and where did Taplin die?"

"My husband was murdered at sea," she said and then she covered her face with her hands.

"Don't ask her any more now," said Packenham pityingly; "let her tell us tomorrow."

She raised her face. "Yes, I will tell you to-morrow. You will take me away with you, will you not, gentlemen--for my child's sake?"

"Of course," said the captain promptly. And he stretched out his honest hand to her.

\* \* \* \*

"She's a wonderfully pretty woman," said Packenham, as we walked the poop later on, and he glanced down through the open skylight to where she and the child slept peacefully on the cushioned transoms. "How prettily she speaks English, too. Do you think she was fond of her husband, or was it merely excitement that made her cry?--native women are as prone to be as hysterical as our own when under any violent emotion."

"I can only tell you, Packenham, that when I saw her last, five years ago, she was a graceful girl of eighteen, and as full of happiness as a bird is of song. She looks thirty now, and her face is thin and drawn--but I don't say all for love of Taplin."

"That will all wear off by and by," said the skipper confidently.

"Yes," I thought, "and she won't be a widow long."

\* \* \* \*

Next morning Nerida had an hour or two among the prints and muslin in the trade-room, and there was something of the old beauty about her when she sat down to breakfast with us. We were to sail at noon. The leak had been stopped, and Packenham was in high good-humour.

"Nerida," I inquired unthinkingly, "do you know what became of the ALIDA? She never turned up again."

"Yes," she answered; "she is here, at the bottom of the lagoon. Will you come and look at her?"

After breakfast we lowered the dingy, the captain and I pulling. Nerida steered us out to the north end of the lagoon till we reached a spot where the water suddenly deepened. It was, in fact, a deep pool, some three or four hundred feet in diameter, closed in by a continuous wall of coral rock, the top of which, even at low water, would be perhaps two or three fathoms under the surface.

She held up her hands for us to back water, then she gazed over the side into the water.

"Look," she said, "there lies the ALIDA."

\* \* \* \*

We bent over the side of the boat. The waters of the lagoon were as smooth as glass and as clear. We saw two slender rounded columns that seemed to shoot up in a slanting direction from out the vague, blue depths beneath, to within four or five fathoms of the surface of the water. Swarms of gorgeously-hued fish swam and circled in and about the masses of scarlet and golden weed that clothed the columns from their tops downward, and swayed gently to and fro as they glided in and out.

A hawk-bill turtle, huge, black, and misshapen, slid out from beneath the dark ledge of the reef, and swam slowly across the pool, and then, between the masts, sank to the bottom.

"'Twas six years ago," said Nerida, as we raised our heads.

That night, as the PALESTINE sped noiselessly before the trade wind to the westward she told me, in the old Funafuti tongue, the tragedy of the ALIDA.

\* \* \* \*

"The schooner," she said, "sailed very quickly, for on the fifteenth day out from Funafuti we saw the far-off peaks of Strong's Island. I was glad, for Kusaie is not many days' sail from Ponape--and I hated to be on the ship. The man with the blue eyes filled me with fear when he looked at me; and he and the captain and mate were for ever talking amongst themselves in whispers.

"There were five native sailors on board--two were countrymen of mine, and three were Tafitos [Natives of the Gilbert Islands].

"One night we were close to a little island called Mokil [Duperrey's Island],and

Taplin and I were awakened by a loud cry on deck; my two countrymen were calling on him to help them. He sprang on deck, pistol in hand, and, behold! the schooner was laid to the wind with the land close to, and the boat alongside, and the three white men were binding my country-men with ropes, because they would not get into the boat.

"'Help us, O friend!' they called to my husband in their own tongue; 'the white men say that if we go not ashore here at Mokil they will kill us. Help us--for they mean evil to thee and Nerida. He with the yellow moustache wants her for his wife.'

"There were quick, fierce words, and then my husband struck Motley on the head with his pistol and felled him, and then pointed it at the mate and the captain, and made them untie the men, and called to the two Tafito sailors who were in the boat to let her tow astern till morning.

"His face was white with the rage that burned in him, and all that night he walked to and fro and let me sleep on the deck near him.

"'To-morrow,' he said, 'I will make this captain land us on Mokil;' it was for that he would not let the sailors come up from the boat.

"At dawn I slept soundly. Then I awoke with a cry of fear, for I heard a shot, and then a groan, and my husband fell across me, and the blood poured out of his mouth and ran down my arms and neck. I struggled to rise, and he tried to draw his pistol, but the man with yellow hair and blue eyes, who stood over him, stabbed him twice in the back. Then the captain and mate seized him by the arms and lifted him up. As his head fell back I saw there was blood streaming from a hole in his chest."

She ceased, and leant her cheek against the face of the little girl, who looked in childish wonder at the tears that streamed down her mother's face.

\* \* \* \*

"They cast him over into the sea with life yet in him, and ere he sank, Motley (that devil with the blue eyes) stood with one foot on the rail and fired another shot, and laughed when he saw the bullet strike. Then he and the other two talked.

"'Let us finish these Pelew men, ere mischief come of it,' said Riedermann, the captain.

"But the others dissuaded him. There was time enough, they said, to kill them. And if they killed them now, there would be but three sailors to work the ship. And Motley looked at me and laughed, and said he, for one, would do no sailor's work yet awhile.

"Then they all trooped below, and took me with them--me, with my husband's blood not yet dried on my hands and bosom. They made me get liquor for them to drink, and they drank and laughed, and Motley put his bloodied hand around my waist and kissed me, and the others laughed still more.

"In a little while Riedermann and the mate were so drunken that no words came from them, and they fell on the cabin floor. Then Motley, who could stand, but staggered as he walked, came and sat beside me and kissed me again, and said he had always loved me; but I pointed to the blood of my husband that stained my skin and clotted my hair together, and besought him to first let me wash it away.

"'Wash it there,' he said, and pointed to his cabin.

"'Nay,' said I, 'see my hair. Let me then go on deck, and I can pour water over my head.'

"But he held my hand tightly as we came up, and my heart died within me; for it was in my mind to spring overboard and follow my husband.

"He called to one of the Tafito men to bring water, but none came; for they, too, were drunken with liquor they had stolen from the hold, where there was plenty in red cases and white cases--gin and brandy. "But my two countrymen were sober; one of them steered the ship, and the other stood beside him with an axe in his hand, for they feared the Tafito men, who are devils when they drink grog.

"'Get some water,' said Motley, to Juan--he who held the axe; and as he brought it, he said, 'How is it, tattooed dog, that thou art so slow to move?' and he struck him in the teeth, and as he struck he fell.

"Ah! that was my time! Ere he could rise I sprang at him, and Juan raised the axe and struck off his right foot; and then Liro, the man who steered, handed me his knife. It was a sharp knife, and I stabbed him, even as he had stabbed my husband, till my arm was tired, and all my hate of him had died away in my heart.

\* \* \* \*

"There was quick work then. My two countrymen went below into the cabin and took Motley's pistol from the table; . . . then I heard two shots.

"GUK! He was a fat, heavy man, that Riedermann, the captain; the three of us could scarce drag him up on deck and cast him over the side, with the other two.

"Then Juan and Liro talked, and said: 'Now for these Tafito men; they, too, must die.' They brought up rifles, and went to the forepart of the schooner, where the Tafito men lay in a drunken sleep, and shot them dead.

"In two more days we saw land--the island we have left but now, and because that there were no people living there--only empty houses could we see--Juan and Liro sailed the schooner into the lagoon.

"We took such things on shore as we needed, and then Juan and Liro cut away the topmasts and towed the schooner to the deep pool, where they made holes in her, so that she sank, away out of the sight of men.

\* \* \* \*

"Juan and Liro were kind to me, and when my child was born, five months after we landed, they cared for me tenderly, so that I soon became strong and well.

"Only two ships did we ever see, but they passed far-off like clouds upon the sea-rim; and we thought to live and die there by ourselves. Then there came a ship, bringing back the people who had once lived there. They killed Juan and Liro, but let me and the child live. The rest I have told you. . . . How is this captain named? . . . He is a handsome man, and I like him."

\* \* \* \*

We landed Nerida at Yap, in the Western Carolines. A year afterwards, when I left the PALESTINE, I heard that Packenham had given up the sea, was trading in the Pelew Group, and was permanently married, and that his wife was the only survivor of the ill-fated ALIDA.

# THE CHILEAN BLUEJACKET
## A Tale Of Easter Island

Alone, in the most solitary part of the Eastern Pacific, midway between the earthquake-shaken littoral of Chili and Peru, and the thousand palm-clad islets of the Low Archipelago, lies an island of the days "when the world was young." By the lithe-limbed, soft-eyed descendants of the forgotten and mysterious race that once quickened the land, this lonely outlier of the isles of the Southern Seas is called in their soft tongue Rapanui, or the Great Rapa.

\* \* \* \*

A hundred and seventy years ago Roggewein, on the dawn of an Easter Sunday, discerned through the misty, tropic haze the grey outlines of an island under his lee beam, and sailed down upon it.

He landed, and even as the grim and hardy old navigator gazed upon and wondered at the mysteries of the strange island, so this day do the cunning men of science, who, perhaps once in thirty years, go thither in the vain effort to read the secret of an all-but-perished race. And they can tell us but vaguely that the stupendous existing evidences of past glories are of immense and untold age, and show their designers to have been coeval with the builders of the buried cities of Mexico and Peru; beyond that, they can tell us nothing.

Who can solve the problem? What manner of an island king was he who ruled the builders of the great terraced platforms of stone, the carvers of the huge blocks of lava, the hewers-out with rudest tools of the Sphinx-like images of trachyte, whose square, massive, and disdainful faces have for unnumbered centuries gazed upwards and outwards over the rolling, sailless swell of the mid-Pacific?

\* \* \* \*

And the people of Rapa-nui of to-day? you may ask. Search the whole Pacific--from Pylstaart, the southern sentinel of the Friendlies, to the one-time buccaneer-haunted, far-away Pelews; thence eastward through the white-beached coral atolls of the Carolines and Marshalls, and southwards to the cloud-capped Marquesas and the sandy stretches of the Paumotu--and you will find no handsomer men or more graceful women than the light-skinned peqple of Rapa-nui.

\* \* \* \*

Yet are they but the survivors of a race doomed--doomed from the day that Roggewein in his clumsy, high-pooped frigate first saw their land, and marvelled at the imperishable relics of a dead greatness. With smiling faces they welcomed him--a stranger from an unknown, outside world, with cutlass at waist and pistol in hand--as a god; he left them a legacy of civilisation--a hideous and cruel disease that swept through the amiable and unsuspicious race as an epidemic, and slew its thousands, and scaled with the hand of Death and Silence the eager life that had then filled the square houses of lava in many a town from the wave-beaten cliffs of Terano Kau to Ounipu in the west.

\* \* \* \*

Ask of the people now, "Whence came ye? and whose were the hands that fashioned these mighty images and carved upon these stones?" and in their simple manner they will answer, "From Rapa, under the setting sun, came our fathers; and we were then a great people, even as the ONEONE [sand] of the beach. . . . Our Great King was it, he whose name is forgotten by us, that caused these temples and cemeteries and terraces to be built; and it was in his time that the forgotten fathers of our fathers carved from out of the stone of the quarries of Terano Kau the great Silent Faces that gaze for ever upward to the sky. . . . AI-A-AH! . . . But it was long ago. . . . Ah! a great people were we then in those days, and the wild people to the West called us TE TAGATA TE PITO HENUA (the people who live at the end of the world) . . . . and we know no more."

And here the knowledge and traditions of a broken people begin and end.

* * * *

# I

A soft, cool morning in November, 187-. Between Ducie and Pitcairn Islands two American whale-ships cruise lazily along to the gentle breath of the south-east trades, when the look-out from both vessels see a third sail bearing down upon them. In a few hours she is close enough to be recognised as one of the luckiest sperm whalers of the fleet--the brig POCAHONTAS, of Martha's Vineyard.

Within a quarter of mile of the two ships--the NASSAU and the DAGGET--the newcomer backs her foreyard and hauls up her mainsail. A cheer rises from the ships. She wants to "gam," I.E. to gossip. With eager hands four boats are lowered from the two ships, and the captains and second mates of each are soon racing for the POCAHONTAS.

* * * *

The skipper of the brig, after shaking hands with his visitors and making the usual inquiries as to their luck, number of days out from New Bedford, etc., led the way to his cabin, and, calling his Portuguese steward, had liquor and a box of cigars brought out. The captain of the POCAHONTAS was a little, withered-up old man with sharp, deep-set eyes of brightest blue, and had the reputation of possessing the most fiery and excitable temper of any of the captains of the sixty or seventy American whale-ships that in those days cruised the Pacific from the West Coast of

South America to Gaum in the Ladrones.

After drinking some of his potent New England rum with his visitors, and having answered all their queries, the master of the POCAHONTAS inquired if they had seen anything of a Chilian man-of-war further to the eastward. No, they had not.

\* \* \* \*

"Then just settle down, gentlemen, for awhile, and I'll tell you one of the curiousest things that I ever saw or heard of. I've logged partiklars of the whole business, and when I get to Oahu (Honolulu) I mean to nar-rate just all I do know to Father Damon of the Honolulu FRIEND. Thar's nothing like a newspaper fur showin' a man up when he's been up to any onnatural villainy, and thinks no one will ever know anything about it. So just take hold and listen."

The two captains nodded, and he told them this.

\* \* \* \*

Ten days previously, when close in to barren and isolated Sala-y-Gomez, the POCAHONTAS had spoken the Chilian corvette O'HIGGINS, bound from Easter Island to Valparaiso. The captain of the corvette entertained the American master courteously, and explained his ship's presence so far to the eastward, by stating that the Government had instructed him to call at Easter Island, and pick up an Englishman in the Chilian service, who had been sent there to examine and report on the colossal statues and mysterious terraces of that lonely island. The Englishman, as Commander Gallegos said, was a valued servant of the Republic, and had for some years served in its Navy as a surgeon on board EL ALMIRANTE COCHRANE, the flag-ship. He had left Valparaiso in the whale-ship COMBOY with the intention of remaining three months on the island. At the end of that time a war vessel was to call and convey him back to Chili. But in less than two months the Republic was in the throes of a deadly struggle with Peru--here the commander of the O'HIGGINS bowed to the American captain, and, pointing to a huge scar that traversed his bronzed face from temple to chin, said, "in which I had the honour to receive this, and promotion"--and nearly two years had elapsed ere the Government had time to think again of the English scientist and his mission. Peace restored, the O'HIGGINS was ordered to proceed to the island and bring him back; and as the character of the natives was not well known, and it was feared he might have been killed, Commander Gallegos was instructed to execute summary justice upon the people of the island, if such was the case.

But, the Chilian officer said, on reaching the island he had found the natives to be very peaceable and inoffensive, and, although much alarmed at the appearance of his armed landing party from the corvette, they had given him a letter from the Englishman, and had satisfied him that Dr Francis ---- had remained with them for some twelve months only, and had then left the island in a passing whale-ship, and Commander Gallegos, making them suitable presents, bade them good-bye, and steamed away to Valparaiso.

* * * *

This was all the polite little commander had to say, and, after a farewell glass of wine, his visitor rose to go, when the captain of the corvette casually inquired if the POCAHONTAS was likely to call at the island.

"I ask you," he said in his perfect English, "because one of my ship's company deserted there. You, senor, may possibly meet with him there. Yet he is of no value, and he is no sailor, and but a lad. He was very ill most of the time, and this was his first voyage. I took him ashore with me in my boat, as he besought me eagerly to do so, and the little devil ran away and hid, or was hidden by the natives."

"Why didn't you get him back?" asked the captain of the POCAHONTAS.

"That was easy enough, but"--and the commander raised his eyebrows and shrugged his shoulders--"of what use? He was no use to the corvette. Better for him to stay there, and perhaps recover, than to die on board the O'HIGGINS and be thrown to the blue sharks. Possibly, senor, you may find him well, and it may suit you to take him to your good ship, and teach him the business of catching the whale. My trade is to show my crew how to fight, and such as he are of no value for that."

Then the two captains bade each other farewell, and in another hour the redoubtable O'HIGGINS, with a black trail of smoke streaming astern, was ten miles away on her course to Valparaiso.

A week after the POCAHONTAS lay becalmed close in to the lee side of Rapanui, and within sight of the houses of the principal village. The captain, always ready to get a "green" hand, was thinking of the chances of his securing the Chilian deserter, and decided to lower a boat and try. Taking four men with him, he pulled ashore, and landed at the village of Hagaroa.

\* \* \* \*

## II

Some sixty or seventy natives clustered round the boat as she touched the shore. With smiling faces and outstretched hands they surrounded the captain, and pressed upon him their simple gifts of ripe bananas and fish baked in leaves, begging him to first eat a little and then walk with them to Mataveri, their largest village, distant a mile, where preparations were being made to welcome him formally. The skipper, nothing loth, bade his crew not to go too far away in their rambles, and, accompanied by his boatsteerer, was about to set off with the natives, when he remembered the object of his visit, and asked a big, well-made woman, the only native present that could speak English, "Where is the man you hid from the man-of-war?"

\* \* \* \*

There was a dead silence, and for nearly half a minute no one spoke. The keen blue eyes of the American looked from one face to another inquiringly, and then settled on the fat, good-natured features of Varua, the big woman.

Holding her hands, palms upwards, to the captain, she endeavoured to speak, and then, to his astonishment, he saw that her dark eyes were filled with tears. And then, as if moved with some sudden and sorrowful emotion, a number of other women and young girls, murmuring softly in pitying tones, "E MATE! E MATE!" ["Dead! Dead!"] came to his side, and held their hands out to him with the same supplicating gesture.

The captain was puzzled. For all his island wanderings and cruises he had no knowledge of any Polynesian dialect, and the tearful muteness of the fat Varua was still unbroken. At last she placed one hand on his sleeve, and, pointing land-ward with the other, said, in her gentle voice, "Come," and taking his hand in hers, she led the way, the rest of the people following in silence.

For about half a mile they walked behind the captain and his boatsteerer and the woman Varua without uttering a word. Presently Varua stopped, and called out the name of "Taku" in a low voice.

A fine, handsome native, partly clothed in European sailor's dress, stepped apart from the others and came to her.

Turning to the captain, she said, "This is Taku the Sailor. He can speak a little English and much Spanish. I tell him now to come with us, for he has a paper."

Although not understanding the relevancy of her remark, the captain nodded, and then with gentle insistence Varua and the other women urged him on, and they again set out.

* * * *

A few minutes more, and they were at the foot of one of the massive-stoned and ancient PAPAKU, or cemeteries, on the walls of which were a number of huge images carved from trachyte, and representing the trunk of the human body. Some of the figures bore on their heads crowns of red tufa, and the aspect of all was to-wards the ocean. At the foot of the wall of the PAPAKU were a number of prone figures, with hands and arms sculptured in low relief, the outspread fingers clasping the hips.

About a cable length from the wall stood two stone houses--memorials of the olden time--and it was to these that Varua and the two white men, attended now by women only, directed their steps.

* * * *

The strange, unearthly stillness of the place, the low whispers of the women, the array of colossal figures with sphinx-like faces set to the sea, and the unutterable air of sadness that enwrapped the whole scene, overawed even the unimaginative mind of the rough whaling captain, and he experienced a curious feeling of relief when his gentle-voiced guide entered through the open doorway the largest of the two houses, and, in a whisper, bade him follow.

* * * *

A delightful sense of coolness was his first sensation on entering, and then with noiseless step the other women followed and seated themselves on the ground.

Still clasping his hand, Varua led him to the farther end of the house, and pointed to a motionless figure that lay on a couch of mats, covered with a large piece of navy-blue calico. At each side of the couch sat a young native girl, and their dark, luminous eyes, shining star-like from out the wealth of black, glossy hair that fell upon their bronzed shoulders, turned wonderingly upon the stranger who had broken in upon their watch.

* * * *

Motioning the girls aside, Varua released her hold of the white man's hand and drew the cloth from off the figure, and the seaman's pitying glance fell upon the pale, sweet features of a young white girl.

But for the unmistakable pallid hue of death he thought at first that she slept. In the thin, delicate hands, crossed upon her bosom, there was placed, after the manner of those of her faith, a small metal crucifix. Her hair, silky and jet black, was short like a man's, and the exquisitely-modelled features, which even the coldness of death had not robbed of their beauty, showed the Spanish blood that, but a few hours before, had coursed through her veins.

Slowly the old seaman drew the covering over the still features, and, with an unusual emotion stirring his rude nature, he rose, and, followed by Varua, walked outside and sat upon a broken pillar of lava that lay under the wall of the PA-PAKU.

\* \* \* \*

Calling his boatsteerer, he ordered him to return to the beach and go off to the ship with instructions to the mate to have a coffin made as quickly as possible and send it ashore; and then, at a glance from Varua, who smiled a grave approval as she listened to his orders, he followed her and the man she called Taku into the smaller of the two houses.

Round about the inside walls of this ancient dwelling of a forgotten race were placed a number of seamen's chests made of cedar and camphor wood--the LARES and PENATES of most Polynesian houses. The gravelled floor was covered with prettily-ornamented mats of FALA (the screw-palm).

Seating herself, with Taku the Sailor, on the mats, Varua motioned the captain to one of the boxes, and then told him a tale that moved him--rough, fierce, and tyrannical as was his nature--to the deepest pity.

\* \* \* \*

# III

"It is not yet twenty days since the fighting PAHI AFI (steamer) came here, and we of Mataveri saw the boat full of armed men land on the beach at Hagaroa. Filled with fear were we; but yet as we had done no wrong we stood on the beach to welcome. And, ere the armed men had left the boat, we knew them to be the SIPANIOLA from Chili--the same as those that came here ten years ago in three ships, and seized and bound three hundred and six of our men, and carried them away for slaves to the land of the Tae Manu, and of whom none but four ever re-turned to Rapa-nui. And then we trembled again."

(She spoke of the cruel outrage of 1862, when three Peruvian slave-ships took away over three hundred islanders to perish on the guano-fields of the Chincha Islands).

"The chief of the ship was a little man, and he called out to us in the tongue of Chili, 'Have no fear,' and took a little gun from out its case of skin that hung by his side, and giving it to a man in the boat, stepped over to us, and took our hands in his.

"'Is there none among ye that speak my tongue?' he said quickly.

"Now, this man here, Taku the Sailor, speaketh the tongue of Chili, but he feared to tell it, lest they might take him away for a sailor; so he held his lips tight.

"Then I, who for six years dwelt with English people at Tahiti, was pushed for-ward by those behind me and made to talk in English; and lo! the little man spoke in your tongue even as quick as he did in that of Chili. And then he told us that he came for Farani [Frank].

\* \* \* \*

"Now this Farani was a young white man of PERETANIA (England), big and strong. He came to us a year and a half ago. He was rich, and had with him chests filled with presents for us of Rapa-nui; and he told us that he came to live a while among us, and look upon the houses of stone and the Faces of the Silent that gaze out upon the sea. For a year he dwelt with us and became as one of ourselves, and we loved him; and then, because no ship came, he began to weary and be sad. At last a ship--like thine, one that hunts for the whale--came, and Farani called us together, and placed a letter in the hands of the chief at Mataveri, and said: 'If it so be that a ship cometh from Chili, give these my words to the captain, and all will be well.' Then he bade us farewell and was gone.

* * * *

"All this I said in quick words, and then we gave to the little fighting chief the letter Farani had written. When he had counted the words in the letter, he said: 'BUENO, it is well,' and called to his men, and they brought out many gifts for us from the boat--cloth, and garments for men and women, and two great bags of canvas filled with tobacco. AI-A-AH! many presents he gave us--this because of the good words Farani had set down in the letter. Then the little chief said to me, 'Let these my men walk where they list, and I will go with thee to Mataveri and talk with the chief.'

"So the sailors came out of the boats carrying their guns and swords in their hands, but the little chief, whose AVAGUTU (moustache) stuck out on each side of his face like the wings of a flying-fish when it leaps in terror from the mouth of the hungry bonito, spoke angrily, and they laid their guns and swords back in the boats.

"So the sailors went hither and thither with our young men and girls; and, although at that time I knew it not, she, who now is not, was one of them, and walked alone.

"Then I, and Taku the Sailor, and the little sea-chief came to the houses of Mataveri, and he stayed awhile and spoke good words to us. And we, although we fear the men of Chili for the wrong they once did us, were yet glad to listen, for we also are of their faith.

* * * *

"As we talked, there came inside the house a young girl named Temeteri, whom, when Farani had been with us for two months, he had taken for wife; and she bore him a son. But from the day that he had sailed away she became sick with grief; and when, after many months, she told me that Farani had said he would return to her, my heart was heavy, for I know the ways of white men with us women of brown skins. Yet I feared to tell her he lied and would return no more. Now, this girl Temeteri was sought after by a man named Huarani, the son of Heremai, who desired to marry her now that Farani had gone, and he urged her to question the chief of the fighting ship, and ask him if Farani would return.

\* \* \* \*

"So I spoke of Temeteri. He laughed and shook his head, and said: 'Nay, Farani the Englishman will return no more; but yet one so beautiful as she,' and he pointed to Temeteri, 'should have many lovers and know no grief. Let her marry again and forget him, and this is my marriage gift to her,' and he threw a big golden coin upon the mat on which the girl sat.

"She took it in her hand and threw it far out through the doorway with bitter words, and rose and went away to her child.

"Then the little captain went back to the boat and called his men to him, and lo! one was gone. Ah! he was angry, and a great scar that ran down one side of his face grew red with rage. But soon he laughed, and said to us: 'See, there be one of my people hidden away from me. Yet he is but a boy, and sick; and I care not to stay and search for him. Let him be thy care so that he wanders not away and perishes among the broken lava; he will be in good hands among the people of Rapa-nui.' With that he bade us farewell, and in but a little time the great fighting ship had gone away towards the rising sun.

\* \* \* \*

"All that day and the next we searched, but found not him who had hidden away; but in the night of the second day, when it rained heavily, and Taku (who is my brother's son) and I and my two children worked at the making of a KUPEGA (net), he whom we had sought came to the door. And as we looked our hearts were filled with pity, for, as he put out his hands to us, he staggered and fell to the ground.

"So Taku--who is a man of a good heart--and I lifted him up and carried him to a bed of soft mats, and as I placed my hand on his bosom to see if he was dead, lo! it was soft as a woman's, and I saw that the stranger was a young girl!

"I took from her the wet garments and brought warm clothes of MAMOE (blankets), and Taku made a great fire, and we rubbed her cold body and her hands and feet till her life came back to her again, and she sat up and ate a little beaten-up taro. When the night and the dawn touched she slept again.

\* \* \* \*

"The sun was high when the white girl awoke, and fear leapt into her eyes when she saw the house filled with people who came to question Taku and me about the stranger. With them came the girl Temeteri, whose head was still filled with foolish thoughts of Farani, her white lover.

"I went to the strange girl, put my arm around her, and spoke, but though she smiled and answered in a little voice, I understood her not, for I know none of the tongue of Chili. But yet she leaned her head against my bosom, and her eyes that were as big and bright as Fetuaho, the star of the morning, looked up into mine and smiled through their tears.

\* \* \* \*

"There was a creat buzzing of talk among the women. Some came to her and touched her hands and forehead, and said: 'Let thy trembling cease; we of Rapa-nui will be kind to the white girl.'

"And as the people thronged about her and talked, she shook her head and her eyes sought mine, and hot tears splashed upon my hand. Then the mother of Temeteri raised her voice and called to Taku the Sailor, and said: 'O Taku, thou who knowest her tongue, ask her of Farani, my white son, the husband of my daughter.'

\* \* \* \*

"The young girls in the house laughed scornfully at old Pohere, for some of them had loved Farani, who yet had put them all aside for Temeteri, whose beauty exceeded theirs; and so they hated her and laughed at her mother. Then Taku, being pressed by old Pohere, spoke in the tongue of Chili, but not of Temeteri.

"Ah! She sprang to her feet and talked then! and the flying words chased one another from her lips; and these things told she to Taku:-- She had hidden among the broken lava and watched the little captain come back to the boat and bid us farewell. Then when night came she had crept out and gone far over to the great PAPAKU, and lay down to hide again, for she feared the fighting ship might return to seek her. And all that day she lay hidden in the lava till night fell upon her again, and hunger drove her to seek the faces of men. In the rain she all but perished, till God brought her feet to this, my house.

"Then said Taku the Sailor: 'Why didst thou flee from the ship?'

"The white girl put her hands to her face and wept, and said: 'Bring me my jacket.'

"I gave to her the blue sailor's jacket, and from inside of it she took a little flat thing and placed it in her bosom.

\* \* \* \*

"Again said old Pohere to Taku: 'O man of slow tongue, ask her of Farani.' So he asked in this wise:

"'See, O White Girl, that is Pohere, the mother of Temeteri, who bore a son to the white man that came here to look upon the Silent Faces; and because he came from thy land, and because of the heart of Temeteri, which is dried up for love of him, does this foolish old woman ask thee if thou hast seen him; for long months ago he left Rapa-nui. In our tongue we call him Farani.'

\* \* \* \*

"The girl looked at Taku the Sailor, and her lips moved, but no words came. Then from her bosom she took the little flat thing and held it to him, but sickness was in her hand so that it trembled, and that which she held fell to the ground. So Taku stooped and picked it up from where it lay on the mat, and looked, and his eyes blazed, and he shouted out 'AUE!' for it was the face of Farani that looked into his! And as he held it up in his hand to the people, they, too, shouted in wonder; and then the girl Temeteri cast aside those that stood about her, and tore it from his hand and fled.

"'Who is she?' said the white girl, in a weak voice to Taku; 'and why hath she robbed me of that which is dear to me?' and Taku was ashamed, and turned his face away from her because of two things--his heart was sore for Temeteri, who is a blood relation, and was shamed because her white lover had deserted her; and he was full of pity for the white girl's tears. So he said nought.

"The girl raised herself, and her hand caught Taku by the arm, and these were her words: 'O man, for the love of Jesu Christ, tell me what was this woman Temeteri to my husband?'

"Now Taku the Sailor was sore troubled, and felt it hard to hurt her heart, yet he said: 'Was Farani, the Englishman, thy husband?'

"She wept again, 'He was my husband.'

"'Why left he one as fair as thee?' said Taku, in wonder.

"She shook her head. 'I know not, except he loved to look upon strange lands; yet he loved me.'

"'He is a bad man,' said Taku. 'He loved others as well as thee. The girl that fled but now with his picture was wife to him here. He loved her, and she bore him a son.'

"The girl's head fell on my shoulder, and her eyes closed, and she became as dead; and lo! in a little while, as she strove to speak, blood poured from her mouth and ran down over her bosom.

"'It is the hand of Death,' said Taku the Sailor.

* * * *

"Where she now lies, there died she, at about the hour when the people of Vaihou saw the sails of thy ship.

"We have no priest here, for the good father that was here three years ago is now silent [i.e. dead]; yet did Taku and I pray with her. And ere she died she said she would set down some words on paper; so Alrema, my little daughter, hastened to Mataveri, and the chief sent back some paper and VAI TUHI (ink) that had belonged to the good priest. So with weak hand she set down some words, but even as she wrote she rose up and threw out her hands, and called out: 'Francisco! Francisco!' and fell back, and was dead."

* * * *

## IV

The captain of the POCAHONTAS dashed the now fast-falling tears from his eyes, and with his rough old heart swelling with pity for the poor wanderer, took from Taku the sheet of paper on which the heart-broken girl's last words were traced.

Ere he could read it a low murmur of voices outside told him his crew had returned. They carried a rude wooden shell, and then with bared heads the captain and boatsteerer entered the house where she lay.

Again the old man raised the piece of navy blue cloth from off the sweet, sad face, and a heavy tear dropped down upon her forehead. Then, aided by the gentle, sympathetic women, his task was soon finished, and two of his crew entered and carried their burden to its grave. Service there was none--only the prayers and tears of the brown women of Rapa-nui.

\* \* \* \*

Ere he said farewell the captain of the whale-ship placed money in the hands of Varua and Taku. They drew back, hurt and mortified. Seeing his mistake, the seaman desired Varua to give the money to the girl Temeteri.

"Nay, sir," said Varua, "she would but give me bitter words. Even when she who is now silent was not yet cold, Temeteri came to the door of the house where she lay and spat twice on the ground, and taking up gravel in her hand cast it at her, and cursed her in the name of our old heathen gods. And as for money, we here in Rapa-nui need it not. May Christ protect thee on the sea. Farewell!"

\* \* \* \*

The captain of the POCAHONTAS rose and came to the cabin table, and motioning to his guests to fill their glasses, said--

"'Tis a real sad story, gentlemen, and if I should ever run across Doctor Francis, I should talk some to him. But see here. Here is my log; my mate, who is a fancy writist, wrote it at my dictation. I can't show you the letter that the pore creature herself wrote; that I ain't going to show to any one."

The two captains rose and stood beside him, and read the entry in the log of the POCAHONTAS.

"November 28, 187-.

This day I landed at Easter Island, to try and obtain as a 'green' hand a young Chilian seaman who, the captain of the Chilian corvette O'HIGGINS informed me, had run away there. On landing I was shown the body of a young girl, whom the natives stated to be the deserter. She had died that morning. Buried her as decently as circumstances would permit. From a letter she wrote on the morning of her death I learned her name to be Senora Teresa T----. Her husband, Dr Francis T----, was an Englishman in the service of the Chilian Republic. He was sent out on a scientific mission to the island, and his wife followed him in the O'HIGGINS disguised as a blue-jacket. I should take her to have been about nineteen years of age.

"SPENCE ELDRIDGE, MASTER. "MANUAL LEGASPE, 2ND OFFICER. "Brig POCAHONTAS, of Martha's Vineyard, U.S.A."

"Well, that's curious now," said the skipper of the NASSAU; "why, I knew that man. He left the island in the KING DARIUS, of New Bedford, and landed at Ponape in the Caroline Group, whar those underground ruins are at Metalanien Harbour. Guess he wanted to potter around there a bit. But he got inter some sorter trouble among the natives there, an' he got shot."

"Aye," said the captain of the DAGGET, "I remember the affair. I was mate of the JOSEPHINE, and we were lying at Jakoits Harbour when he was killed, and now I remember the name too. Waal, he wasn't much account, anyhow."

\* \* \* \*

Ten years ago a wandering white man stood, with Taku the Sailor, at the base of the wall of the great PAPAKU, and the native pointed out the last resting-place of the wanderer. There, under the shadow of the Silent Faces of Stone, the brave and loving heart that dared so much is at peace for ever.

# BRANTLEY OF VAHITAHI

One day a trading vessel lay becalmed off Tatakoto, in the Paumotu Archipelago, and the captain and supercargo, taking a couple of native sailors with them, went ashore at dawn to catch some turtle. The turtle were plentiful and easily caught, and after half a dozen had been put in the boat, the two white men strolled along the white hard beach. The captain--old, grizzled, and grim--seemed to know the place well, and led the way.

* * * *

The island is very narrow, and as they left the beach and gained the shade of the forest of coconuts that grew to the margin of high-water mark, they could see, between the tall, stately palms, the placid waters of the lagoon, and a mile or so across, the inner beach of the weather side of the island.

For a quarter of a mile or so the two men walked on till the widest part of the island was reached. Here, under the shadow of some giant PUKA trees, the old skipper stopped and sat down on a roughly hewn slab of coral, the remains of one of those MARAE or heathen temples that are to be found almost anywhere in the islands of Eastern Polynesia.

"I knew this place well, once," he said, as he pulled out his pipe. "I used to come here when I was sailing one of Brander's vessels out of Tahiti. As we have done now we did then--came here for turtle. No natives have lived here for the past forty years. Did you ever hear of Brantley?"

"Yes," answered the supercargo, "but he died long ago, did he not?"

"Aye, he died here, and his wife and sister too. They all lie here in this old

MARAE."

And then he told the story of Brantley.

* * * *

# I

It was six years since Brantley, with his companions in misery, had drifted ashore at lonely Vahitahi in the Paumotu Group, and the kindly-hearted people had gazed with pitying horror upon the dreadful beings that, muttering and gibbering to each other, lay in the bottom of the boat, and pointed with long talon-like fingers to their burnt and bloody thirst-tortured lips.

* * * *

And now as he sits in the doorway of his thatched house, and gazes dreamily out upon the long curve of creamy beach and wind-swayed line of palms that fringe the leeward side of his island home, Brantley passes a brown hand slowly up and down his sun-bronzed cheek, and thinks of the past.

He was so full of life--of the very joy of living--that time six years ago when he sailed from Auckland on that fateful voyage in the DORIS. It was his first voyage as captain, and the ship was his own, and even now he remembers with a curious time-dulled pang the last words of his only sister--the Doris after whom he had called his new ship--as she had kissed him farewell--"I am so glad, Fred, to hear them call you 'Captain Brantley.'"

And the voyage--the wild feverish desire to make a record passage to 'Frisco and back; the earnest words of poor old white-headed Lutton, the mate, "not to carry on so at night going through the Paumotu Group"; that awful midnight crash when the DORIS ran hopelessly into the wild boil of roaring surf on Tuanake Reef; the white, despairing faces of five of his men, who, with curses in their eyes upon his folly, were swept out of sight into the awful blackness of the night. And then the days in the boat with the six survivors! Ah! the memory of that will chill his blood to his dying day. Men have had to do that which he and the two who came through alive with him had done.

How long they endured that black agony of suffering he knew not. By common consent none of them ever spoke of it again.

Three months after they had drifted ashore, a passing sperm whaler, cruising through the group, took away the two seamen, and then Brantley, after bidding them a silent farewell, had, with bitter despair gnawing at his heart, turned his face away from the ship, and walked. back into the palm-shaded village.

* * * *

"I will never go back again," he had said to himself. And perhaps he was right; for when the DORIS went to pieces on Tuanake his hope and fortunes went with her, and, save for that other Doris, there was no one in the world who cared for him. He was not the man to face the world again with: "Why, he lost his first ship!" whispered among his acquaintances.

And this is how Brantley--young, handsome, and as smart a seaman (save for that one fatal mistake) as ever trod a deck--became Paranili the PAPALAGI, and was living out his life among the people of solitary Vahitahi.

* * * *

Ere a year had passed a trading captain bound to the Gambier Islands had given him a small stock of trade goods, and the thought of Doris had been his salvation. Only for her he would have sunk to the life of a mere idle, gin-drinking, and dissolute beach-comber. As it was, his steady, straightforward life among the people of the island was a big factor to his business success. And so every year he sent money to Doris by some passing whaler or Tahitian trading schooner, but twice only had he got letters from her; and each time she had said: "Let me come to you, Fred. We are alone in the world, and may never meet again else. Sometimes I awake in the night with a sudden fear. Let me come; my heart is breaking with the loneliness of my life here, so far away from you."

* * * *

But two years ago he had done that which would keep Doris from ever coming to him, he thought. He had married a young native girl--that is, taken her to wife in the Paumotuan fashion--and surely Doris, with her old-fashioned notions of right and wrong, would grieve bitterly if she knew it.

Presently he rose, talking to himself as is the wont of those who have lived long apart from all white associations, and sauntered up and down the shady path at the side of his dwelling, thinking of Doris, and if he would ever see her again. Then he entered the house.

* * * *

Seated on the matted floor with her face turned from him was a young native girl--Luita, his wife. She was making a hat from the bleached strands of the pandanus leaf, and as she worked she sang softly to herself in the semi-Tahitian tongue of her people.

Brantley, lazily stretching himself out on a rough mat-covered couch, turned towards her, and watched the slender, supple fingers--covered, in Polynesian fashion, with heavy gold rings--as they deftly drew out the snow-white strands of the pandanus. The long, glossy, black waves of hair that fell over her bare back and bosom like a mantle of night hid her face from his view, and the man let his glance rest in contented admiration upon the graceful curves of the youthful figure; then he sighed softly, and again his eyes turned to the wide, sailless expanse of the Pacific, that lay shimmering and sparkling before him under a cloudless sky of blue, and he thought again of Doris.

\* \* \* \*

Steadily the little hands worked in and out among the snowy strands, and now and then, as she came to the TARI, or refrain, of the old Paumotuan love-song, her soft liquid tones would blend with the quavering treble of children that played outside.

"Terunavahori, teeth of pearl, Knit the sandals for Talaloo's feet, /L>Sandals of AFA thick and strong, Bind them well with thy long black hair."

Suddenly the song ceased, and with a quick movement of her shoulders she threw back the cloud of hair that fell around her arms and bosom, looked up at Brantley and laughed, and, striking the mat on which she sat with her open palm, said--

"HAERE MAI, PARANILI."

He rose from the couch and stooped beside her, with his hands resting on his knees, and bending his brow in mock criticism, regarded her handiwork intently.

Springing to her feet, hat in hand, and placing her two hands on his now erect shoulders, she looked into his face--darker far than her own--and said with a smile--

"Behold, Paranili, thy PULOU is finished, save for a band of black PU'AVA which thou shalt give me from the store."

"Mine?" said Brantley, in pretended ignorance. "Why labour so for me? Are there not hats in plenty on Vahitahi?"

"True, O thankless one! but the women of the village say that thou lookest upon me as a fool because I can neither make mats nor do many other things such as becometh a wife. And for this did Merani, my cousin, teach me how to make a wide hat of FALA to shield thy face from the sun when thou art out upon the pearl-ing grounds. AI-E-EH! my husband, but thy face and neck and hands are as dark as those of the people of Makatea--they who are for ever in their canoes. . . . See, Paranili, bend thy head. AI-E-EH! thou art a tall man, my husband," and she trilled a happy, rippling laugh as she placed the hat on his head.

He placed one hand around the pliant waist and under the mantle of hair, and drew her towards him, and then, moved by a sudden emotion, kissed her soft, red lips.

"Luita," he asked, "would it hurt thee if I were to go away?"

The girl drew away from him, and, for the first time in two years Brantley saw an angry flush tinge her cheek a dusky red.

\* \* \* \*

"Ah!"--the contemptuous ring in her voice made the man's eyes drop--"thou art like all White Men--was there ever one who was faithful? What other woman is it that thou desirest? Is it Nia of Ahunui--she who, when thy boat lay anchored in the lagoon, swam off at night and asked thee for thy love--the shameless Nia?"

The angry light in the black eyes shone fiercely, and the dull red on her cheeks had changed to the livid paleness of passion.

Brantley, holding the rim of the hat over his mouth, laughed secretly, pleased at her first outburst of jealousy. Then his natural manliness asserted itself.

"Come here," he said.

Somewhat sullenly the girl obeyed and edged up beside him with face bent down. He put his hand upon hers, and for a few seconds looked at the delicate tracery of tattooing that, on the back, ran in thin blue lines from the finger tips to the wrists.

"What a d----d pity!" he muttered to himself; "this infernal tattooing would give the poor devil away anywhere in civilization. Her skin is not as dark as that pretty creole I was so sweet on in Galveston ten years ago . . . Well, she's good enough for a broken man like me--but I can't take her away--that's certain."

A heavy tear splashed on his hand, and then he pulled her to him, almost savagely.

"See, Luita. I did but ask to try thee. Have no fear. Thy land is mine for ever."

The girl looked up, and in an instant her face, wet with tears, was laid against his breast. Still caressing the dark head that lay upon his chest, Brantley stooped and whispered something. The little tattooed hand released its clasp of his arm and struck him a playful blow.

"And would that bind thee more to me, and to the ways of these our people of Vahitahi," she asked, with still buried face.

"Aye," answered the ex-captain slowly, "for I have none but thee in the world to care for."

She turned her face up. "Is there none--not even one woman in far-off Beretania, whose face comes to thee in the darkness."

Brantley shook his head sadly. Of course there was Doris, he thought, but he had never spoken of her. Sometimes when the longing to see her again would come upon him, he would have talked of her to his native wife, but he was by nature an uncommunicative man, and the thought of how Doris must feel her loneliness touched him with remorse and made him silent.

\* \* \* \*

Another year passed, and matters had gone well with Brantley. Ten months before he had dropped on one of the best patches of shell in the Paumotus, and to-day, as he sits writing and smoking in the big room of his house, he looks contentedly out through the open door to a little white painted schooner that lay at anchor on the calm waters of the lagoon. He had just come back from Tahiti with her, and the two thousand dollars he had paid for the vessel was an easy matter for a man who was now making a thousand dollars a month.

"What a stroke of luck!" he writes to Doris. "Had I gone back to Sydney, where would I be now?--a mate, I suppose, on some deep-sea ship, earning twelve or fourteen pounds a month. Another year or two like this, and I can go back a made man. Some day, my dear, I may; but I will come back here again. The ways of the people have become my ways."

\* \* \* \*

He laid down his pen and came to the door, and stood thinking awhile and listening to the gentle rustle of the palms as they swayed their lofty plumes to the breezy trade wind.

"Yes," he thought, "I would like to go and see Doris, but I can't take Luita, and so it cannot be. How that girl suspects me even now. When I went to Tahiti to buy the schooner, I believe she thought she would never see me again.... What a fool I am! Doris is all right, I suppose, although it is a year since I had a letter . . . and I--could any man want more. I don't believe there's a soul on the island but thinks as much of me as Luita herself does; and, by G-d! she's a pearl--even though she is only a native girl. No, I'll stay here; 'Kapeni Paranili' will always be a big man in the Pau-motus, but Fred Brantley would be nobody in Sydney--only a common merchant skipper who had made money in the islands. . . . And perhaps Doris is married."

\* \* \* \*

So he thought and talked to himself, listening the while to the soft symphony of the swaying palm-tops and the subdued murmur of the surf as the rollers crashed on the distant line of reef away to leeward. Of late these fleeting visions of the outside world--that quick, busy world, whose memories, save for those of Doris, were all but dead to him--had become more frequent; but the calm, placid happiness of his existence, and that strange, fatal glamour that for ever enwraps the minds of those who wander in the islands of the sunlit sea--as the old Spanish navigators called Polynesia--had woven its spell too strongly over his nature to be broken. And now, as the murmur of women's voices caused him to turn his head to the shady end of the verandah, the dark, dreamy eyes of Luita, who with her women attendants sat there playing with her child, looked out at him from beneath their long lashes, and told him his captivity was complete.

\* \* \* \*

A week afterwards the people of Vahitahi were clustered on the beach putting supplies of native food in the schooner's boat. That night he was to sail again for the pearling grounds at Matahiva lagoon, and would be away three months.

One by one the people bade him adieu, and then stood apart while he said farewell to Luita.

"E MAHINA TOLU [Only three months], little one," he said, "why such a gloomy face?"

The girl shook her head, and her mouth twitched. "But the MITI [dream], Paranili--the MITI of my mother. She is wise in the things that are hidden; for she is one of those who believe in the old gods of Vahitahi. . . . And there are many here of the new LOTU [Faith, i.e. Christianity] who yet believe in the old gods. And, see, she has dreamed of this unknown evil to thee twice; and twice have the voices of those who are silent in the MARAE called to me in the night, and said: 'He must not go; he must not go.'"

Knowing well how the old superstitious taint ran riot in the imaginative native mind, Brantley did not attempt to reason, but sought to gently disengage her hands from his arm.

She dropped on the sand at his feet and clasped his knees, and a long, wailing note of grief rang out--

"AUE! AUE! my husband! if it so be that thou dost not heed the voices that call in the night, then, out of thy love for me and our child, let me come also. Then, if evil befall thee, let us perish together."

Brantley raised his hand and pointed to the bowed and weeping figure. Some women came and lifted her up. Then taking the tender face between his rough hands, he bent his head to hers, sprang into the boat, and was gone.

* * * *

## II

With ten tons of shell snugly stowed in her hold, the little Tamariki was head-ing back for Vahitahi after barely two months' absence. Brantley, as he leant over the rail and watched the swirl and eddy of the creamy phosphorescence that hissed and bubbled under the vessel's stern, felt well satisfied.

It was the hour of dawn, and the native at the tiller sang, as the stars began to pale before the red flush that tinged the sky to windward, a low chant of farewell to Fetuaho, the star of the morning, and then he called to Brantley, who to all his crew was always "Paranili," and never "Kapeni [Captain]," and pointed with his naked, tattooed arm away to leeward, where the low outlines of an island began to show.

"Look, Paranili, that is Tatakoto, the place I have told thee of, where the turtle makes the white beach to look black. Would it not be well for us to take some home to Vahitahi?"

"Thou glutton!" said Brantley, good-humouredly, "dost thou think I am like to lose a day so that thou and thy friends may fill thy stomachs with turtle meat?"

Rua Manu laughed, and showed his white, even teeth. "Nay, Paranili, not for that alone; but it is a great place, that Tatakoto, and thou hast never landed there to look, and Luita hath said that some day she would ask thee to take her there; for, though she was born at Vahitahi, her blood is that of the people of Tatakoto, who have long since lain silent in the MARAES."

* * * *

Brantley had often heard her speak of it, this solitary spot in the wide Pacific, and now, as he looked at the pretty, verdure-clad island against the weather shore of which the thundering rollers burst with a muffled roar, he was surprised at its length and extent, and decided to pay it a visit some day.

"Not now, Rua," he said to the steersman, "but it shall be soon. Are there many coconuts there?"

"Many? May I perish, but the trees are as the sand of the sea, and the nuts lie thick upon the ground. AI-E-EH! and the robber crabs are in thousands, and fat; and the sea-birds' eggs!"

"Glutton again! Be content. In a little while we and as many of the people of Vahitahi as the schooner will carry will go there and stay for the turtle season."

\* \* \* \*

Three days afterwards the schooner was within fifty miles of his island home, when Brantley was aroused at daylight from his watch below by the cry of "TE PAHI!" (a ship!) and hastening on deck he saw a large vessel bearing down upon them. In half an hour she was close to, and Brantley recognised her as a brig from Tahiti, that occasionally made a trading voyage to the Paumotus, and whose skipper was a personal friend. Suddenly she hove-to and lowered a boat, which came alongside the schooner, and the white man that steered jumped on deck and held out his hand.

"How are you, Brantley?" and then his eye went quickly over the crew of the schooner, then glanced through the open skylight into the little cabin, and a hopeful, expectant look in his face died away.

"Very well, thank you, Latham. But what is wrong?--you look worried."

"Come on board," said the captain of the brig, quietly, "and I'll tell you."

As Brantley took his seat beside him, Latham said: "I have bad news for you, Brantley. Your sister is on board the brig, and I fear she will not live long. She came down to Tahiti in the MARAMA from Auckland, and offered me a good round sum to bring her to you."

"Has she been ill long, Latham?"

* * * *

Latham looked at him curiously. "Didn't you know, Brantley? She's in a rapid consumption."

For a moment neither men spoke; then Latham gave a short cough.

"I feel it almost as badly as you, Brantley--but I've got a bit more bad news--"

"Go on, Latham--it can't matter much. My poor sister is everything to me."

"Just so. That's what I told Miss Brantley. Well, it's this--your wife and child are missing----" Latham glanced at him and saw that his hand trembled and then grasped the gunwale of the boat.

"We got into Vahitahi lagoon about ten days ago, and I took Miss Brantley ashore. What happened I don't exactly know, but the next night one of your whale-boats was gone, and Luita and the child were missing. Your sister was in a terrible state of mind, and offered me a thousand dollars to put to sea. Brantley, old man, I wouldn't take a dollar from her--God bless her--but I did put to sea, and I've searched nigh on twenty islands, and scores of reefs and sandbanks----"

"Thank you, Latham," said Brantley quietly; "when we get on board you can give me further particulars of the islands you've searched."

"You can have my marked chart; I've got a spare one. Brace up, old man! you'll see your sister in a minute. She is terribly cut up over poor Luita--more so than I knew you would be. But she was a grand little woman, Brantley, although she was only a native."

"Yes," he answered, in the same slow, dazed manner, "she was a good little girl to me, although she----" The words stuck in his throat.

* * * *

Latham showed him into the brig's cabin, and then a door opened, and Doris threw herself weeping into his arms.

"Oh, Doris," he whispered, "why did you not tell me you were ill? I would have come to you long ago. I feel a brute----"

She placed her hand on his lips. "Never mind about me, Fred. Has Captain Latham told you about----"

"Yes," he replied; and then suddenly: "Doris, I am going to look for her; I think I know the place to which she has gone. It is not far from here. Doris, will you go on back to Vahitahi with Latham and wait for me?"

"Fred," she whispered, "let me come with you. It will not be long, dear, before I am gone, and it was hard to die away from you--that is why I came; and perhaps we may find her."

He kissed her silently, and then in five minutes more they had said farewell to Latham, and were on their way to the schooner.

The crew soon knew from him what had happened, and Rua Manu, with his big eyes filled with a wondering pity as he looked at the frail body and white face of Doris lying on the skylight, wore the schooner's head round to the south-west at a sign from Brantley.

"Aye, Paranili," he said, in his deep, guttural tones, "it is to Tatakoto she hath gone--'tis her mother's land."

\* \* \* \*

That night, as she lay on the skylight with her hand in his, Doris told him all she knew:--

"They were all kind to me when I went ashore to your house, Fred, but Luita looked so fiercely at me. . . . Her eyes frightened me--they had a look of death in them.

"In the morning your little child was taken ill with what they call TATARU, and I wanted to give it medicine. Luita pushed my hand away and hugged the child to her bosom; and then the other women came and made signs for me to go away. And that night she and the child were missing, and one of your boats was gone."

"Poor Luita," said Brantley, stroking Doris's pale cheek, "she did not know you were my sister. I never told her, Doris."

"She is a very beautiful woman, Fred. They told me at Tahiti that she was called the pearl of Vahitahi; and oh! my dear, if we can but find her, I will make her love me for your sake."

\* \* \* \*

Late in the afternoon of the second day, just as the trade wind began to lose its strength, the schooner was running along the weather-side of Tatakoto, and Rua Manu, from the mast-head, called out that he saw the boat lying on the beach inside the lagoon, with her sail set; and, as landing was not practicable on the weather-side, the schooner ran round to the lee.

"We will soon know, Doris. It always rains in these islands at this time of the year, so she would not suffer as I once did; but the sail of the boat is still set, and that makes me think she has never left it. Wait till I come back again, Doris; you cannot help me."

And Doris, throwing her weak arms round his neck, kissed him with a sob, and lay back again to wait.

\* \* \* \*

With Rua Manu and two others of his faithful native crew, Brantley walked quickly across the island to the lagoon to where the boat lay. Luita was not there, and the dark eyes of his sailors met his in a responsive glow of hope--she had not died in the boat!

They turned back into the silent aisles of coconut palms, and then Rua Manu loudly called her name.

"Listen," he said.

A voice--a weak, trembling voice--was singing the song of Talaloo.

"Terunavahori, bending low, Bindeth the sandals on Talaloo's feet; 'Hasten, O hasten, lover true, O'er the coral, cruel and sharp, Over the coral, and sand, and rock, Snare thee a turtle for our marriage feast; IA AKOE! brave lover mine.'"

"In the old MARAE, Paranili," said Rua Manu, pointing to the remains of a ruined temple. Motioning to the seamen to remain outside, Brantley entered the crumbling walls of the old heathen MARAE. At the far end was a little screen of coconut boughs. He stooped down and went in.

A few minutes passed, and then his hand was thrust out between the branches as a sign for them to follow.

* * * *

One by one they came and sat beside Brantley, who held the wasted figure of the wanderer in his arms. The sound of his voice had brought back her wavering reason, and she knew them all now. She knew, too, that her brief young life was ebbing fast; for, as each of the brown men pressed their lips to her hand, tears coursed down their cheeks.

"See, men of Vahitahi, my Englishman hath come to me, a fool that fled from his house . . . because I thought that he lied to me. Teloma was it who first mocked, and said: ''Tis his wife from Beretania who hath come to seek him;' and then other girls laughed and mocked also, and said: 'AH-HE! Luita, this fair-faced girl who sayeth she is thy husband's sister, AH-HE!' . . . and their words and looks stung me . . . So at night I took my child and swam to the boat. . . . My child, see, it is here," and she touched a little mound in the soil beside her.

There was a low murmur of sympathy, and then the brown men went outside and covered their faces with their hands, after the manner of their race when death is near, and waited in silence.

* * * *

Night had fallen on the lonely island, and the far-off muffled boom of the breakers as they dashed on the black ledges of the weather reef would now and then be borne into the darkness of the little hut.

"Put thy face to mine, Paranili," she whispered; "I grow cold now."

As the bearded face of the man bent over her, one thin, weak arm rose waveringly in the air, and then fell softly round his neck, and Brantley, with his hand upon her bosom, felt that her heart had ceased to beat.

\* \* \* \*

The next day he sailed the schooner into the lagoon, and Doris pressed her lips on the dead forehead of the native girl ere she was laid to rest. Something that Doris had said to him as they walked away from her grave filled Brantley's heart with a deadly fear, and as he took her in his arms his voice shook.

"Don't say that, Doris. It cannot be so soon as that. I was never a good man; but surely God will spare you to me a little longer."

But it came very soon--on the morning of the day that he intended sailing out of the lagoon again, Doris died in his arms on board the schooner, and Brantley laid her to rest under the shade of a giant puka-tree that overshadowed the stones of the old MARAE.

\* \* \* \*

That night he called Rua Manu into the cabin and asked him if he could beat his way back to Vahitahi in the schooner.

"'Tis an easy matter, Paranili. So that the sky be clear and I can see the stars, then shall I find Vahitahi in three days."

"Good. Then to-morrow take the schooner there, and tell such of the people as desire to be with me to come here, and bring with them all things that are in my house. It is my mind to live here at Tatakoto."

As the schooner slipped through the narrow passage, he stood on the low, sandy point, and waved his hand in farewell.

\* \* \* \*

A week later the little vessel dropped her anchor in the lagoon again, and Rua Manu and his crew came ashore to seek him.

They found him lying under the shade of the puka-tree with his revolver in his hand and a bullet-hole in his temple.

### The Codes Of Hammurabi And Moses
### W. W. Davies

QTY

The discovery of the Hammurabi Code is one of the greatest achievements of archaeology, and is of paramount interest, not only to the student of the Bible, but also to all those interested in ancient history...

**Religion**     **ISBN:** *1-59462-338-4*        **Pages:132**
*MSRP $12.95*

### The Theory of Moral Sentiments
### Adam Smith

QTY

This work from 1749. contains original theories of conscience amd moral judgment and it is the foundation for systemof morals.

**Philosophy**   **ISBN:** *1-59462-777-0*        **Pages:536**
*MSRP $19.95*

### Jessica's First Prayer
### Hesba Stretton

QTY

In a screened and secluded corner of one of the many railway-bridges which span the streets of London there could be seen a few years ago, from five o'clock every morning until half past eight, a tidily set-out coffee-stall, consisting of a trestle and board, upon which stood two large tin cans, with a small fire of charcoal burning under each so as to keep the coffee boiling during the early hours of the morning when the work-people were thronging into the city on their way to their daily toil...

**Pages:84**

**Childrens**   **ISBN:** *1-59462-373-2*        *MSRP $9.95*

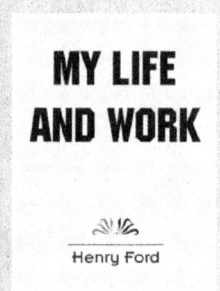

### My Life and Work
### Henry Ford

QTY

Henry Ford revolutionized the world with his implementation of mass production for the Model T automobile.  Gain valuable business insight into his life and work with his own auto-biography... "We have only started on our development of our country we have not as yet, with all our talk of wonderful progress, done more than scratch the surface. The progress has been wonderful enough but..."

**Pages:300**

**Biographies/**   **ISBN:** *1-59462-198-5*        *MSRP $21.95*

## The Art of Cross-Examination
## Francis Wellman

I presume it is the experience of every author, after his first book is published upon an important subject, to be almost overwhelmed with a wealth of ideas and illustrations which could readily have been included in his book, and which to his own mind, at least, seem to make a second edition inevitable. Such certainly was the case with me; and when the first edition had reached its sixth impression in five months, I rejoiced to learn that it seemed to my publishers that the book had met with a sufficiently favorable reception to justify a second and considerably enlarged edition. ...

QTY

Reference     ISBN: *1-59462-647-2*

Pages:412

*MSRP $19.95*

## On the Duty of Civil Disobedience
## Henry David Thoreau

Thoreau wrote his famous essay, On the Duty of Civil Disobedience, as a protest against an unjust but popular war and the immoral but popular institution of slave-owning. He did more than write—he declined to pay his taxes, and was hauled off to gaol in consequence. Who can say how much this refusal of his hastened the end of the war and of slavery ?

QTY

Law          ISBN: *1-59462-747-9*

Pages:48

*MSRP $7.45*

## Dream Psychology Psychoanalysis for Beginners
## Sigmund Freud

Sigmund Freud, born Sigismund Schlomo Freud (May 6, 1856 - September 23, 1939), was a Jewish-Austrian neurologist and psychiatrist who co-founded the psychoanalytic school of psychology. Freud is best known for his theories of the unconscious mind, especially involving the mechanism of repression; his redefinition of sexual desire as mobile and directed towards a wide variety of objects; and his therapeutic techniques, especially his understanding of transference in the therapeutic relationship and the presumed value of dreams as sources of insight into unconscious desires.

QTY

Dream Psychology
Psychoanalysis for Beginners

Sigmund Freud

Psychology     ISBN: *1-59462-905-6*

Pages:196

*MSRP $15.45*

## The Miracle of Right Thought
## Orison Swett Marden

Believe with all of your heart that you will do what you were made to do. When the mind has once formed the habit of holding cheerful, happy, prosperous pictures, it will not be easy to form the opposite habit. It does not matter how improbable or how far away this realization may see, or how dark the prospects may be, if we visualize them as best we can, as vividly as possible, hold tenaciously to them and vigorously struggle to attain them, they will gradually become actualized, realized in the life. But a desire, a longing without endeavor, a yearning abandoned or held indifferently will vanish without realization.

QTY

Self Help       ISBN: *1-59462-644-8*

Pages:360

*MSRP $25.45*

www.**bookjungle**.com *email: sales@bookjungle.com fax: 630-214-0564 mail: Book Jungle PO Box 2226 Champaign, IL 61825*

QTY

**The Rosicrucian Cosmo-Conception Mystic Christianity** by *Max Heindel*    ISBN: *1-59462-188-8*    **$38.95**
*The Rosicrucian Cosmo-conception is not dogmatic, neither does it appeal to any other authority than the reason of the student. It is: not controversial, but is: sent forth in the, hope that it may help to clear...*    New Age/Religion Pages 646

**Abandonment To Divine Providence** by *Jean-Pierre de Caussade*    ISBN: *1-59462-228-0*    **$25.95**
*"The Rev. Jean Pierre de Caussade was one of the most remarkable spiritual writers of the Society of Jesus in France in the 18th Century. His death took place at Toulouse in 1751. His works have gone through many editions and have been republished...*    Inspirational/Religion Pages 400

**Mental Chemistry** by *Charles Haanel*    ISBN: *1-59462-192-6*    **$23.95**
*Mental Chemistry allows the change of material conditions by combining and appropriately utilizing the power of the mind. Much like applied chemistry creates something new and unique out of careful combinations of chemicals the mastery of mental chemistry...*    New Age Pages 354

**The Letters of Robert Browning and Elizabeth Barret Barrett 1845-1846 vol II**    ISBN: *1-59462-193-4*    **$35.95**
by *Robert Browning* and *Elizabeth Barrett*    Biographies Pages 596

**Gleanings In Genesis (volume I)** by *Arthur W. Pink*    ISBN: *1-59462-130-6*    **$27.45**
*Appropriately has Genesis been termed "the seed plot of the Bible" for in it we have, in germ form, almost all of the great doctrines which are afterwards fully developed in the books of Scripture which follow...*    Religion/Inspirational Pages 420

**The Master Key** by *L. W. de Laurence*    ISBN: *1-59462-001-6*    **$30.95**
*In no branch of human knowledge has there been a more lively increase of the spirit of research during the past few years than in the study of Psychology, Concentration and Mental Discipline. The requests for authentic lessons in Thought Control, Mental Discipline and...*    New Age/Business Pages 422

**The Lesser Key Of Solomon Goetia** by *L. W. de Laurence*    ISBN: *1-59462-092-X*    **$9.95**
*This translation of the first book of the "Lernegton" which is now for the first time made accessible to students of Talismanic Magic was done, after careful collation and edition, from numerous Ancient Manuscripts in Hebrew, Latin, and French...*    New Age/Occult Pages 92

**Rubaiyat Of Omar Khayyam** by *Edward Fitzgerald*    ISBN:*1-59462-332-5*    **$13.95**
*Edward Fitzgerald, whom the world has already learned, in spite of his own efforts to remain within the shadow of anonymity, to look upon as one of the rarest poets of the century, was born at Bredfield, in Suffolk, on the 31st of March, 1809. He was the third son of John Purcell...*    Music Pages 172

**Ancient Law** by *Henry Maine*    ISBN: *1-59462-128-4*    **$29.95**
*The chief object of the following pages is to indicate some of the earliest ideas of mankind, as they are reflected in Ancient Law, and to point out the relation of those ideas to modern thought.*    Religion/History Pages 452

**Far-Away Stories** by *William J. Locke*    ISBN: *1-59462-129-2*    **$19.45**
*"Good wine needs no bush, but a collection of mixed vintages does. And this book is just such a collection. Some of the stories I do not want to remain buried for ever in the museum files of dead magazine-numbers an author's not unpardonable vanity..."*    Fiction Pages 272

**Life of David Crockett** by *David Crockett*    ISBN: *1-59462-250-7*    **$27.45**
*"Colonel David Crockett was one of the most remarkable men of the times in which he lived. Born in humble life, but gifted with a strong will, an indomitable courage, and unremitting perseverance...*    Biographies/New Age Pages 424

**Lip-Reading** by *Edward Nitchie*    ISBN: *1-59462-206-X*    **$25.95**
*Edward B. Nitchie, founder of the New York School for the Hard of Hearing, now the Nitchie School of Lip-Reading, Inc, wrote "LIP-READING Principles and Practice". The development and perfecting of this meritorious work on lip-reading was an undertaking...*    How-to Pages 400

**A Handbook of Suggestive Therapeutics, Applied Hypnotism, Psychic Science**    ISBN: *1-59462-214-0*    **$24.95**
by *Henry Munro*    Health/New Age/Health/Self-help Pages 376

**A Doll's House: and Two Other Plays** by *Henrik Ibsen*    ISBN: *1-59462-112-8*    **$19.95**
*Henrik Ibsen created this classic when in revolutionary 1848 Rome. Introducing some striking concepts in playwriting for the realist genre, this play has been studied the world over.*    Fiction/Classics/Plays 308

**The Light of Asia** by *sir Edwin Arnold*    ISBN: *1-59462-204-3*    **$13.95**
*In this poetic masterpiece, Edwin Arnold describes the life and teachings of Buddha. The man who was to become known as Buddha to the world was born as Prince Gautama of India but he rejected the worldly riches and abandoned the reigns of power when...*    Religion/History/Biographies Pages 170

**The Complete Works of Guy de Maupassant** by *Guy de Maupassant*    ISBN: *1-59462-157-8*    **$16.95**
*"For days and days, nights and nights, I had dreamed of that first kiss which was to consecrate our engagement, and I knew not on what spot I should put my lips..."*    Fiction/Classics Pages 240

**The Art of Cross-Examination** by *Francis L. Wellman*    ISBN: *1-59462-309-0*    **$26.95**
*Written by a renowned trial lawyer, Wellman imparts his experience and uses case studies to explain how to use psychology to extract desired information through questioning.*    How-to/Science/Reference Pages 408

**Answered or Unanswered?** by *Louisa Vaughan*    ISBN: *1-59462-248-5*    **$10.95**
*Miracles of Faith in China*    Religion Pages 112

**The Edinburgh Lectures on Mental Science (1909)** by *Thomas*    ISBN: *1-59462-008-3*    **$11.95**
*This book contains the substance of a course of lectures recently given by the writer in the Queen Street Hall, Edinburgh. Its purpose is to indicate the Natural Principles governing the relation between Mental Action and Material Conditions...*    New Age/Psychology Pages 148

**Ayesha** by *H. Rider Haggard*    ISBN: *1-59462-301-5*    **$24.95**
*Verily and indeed it is the unexpected that happens! Probably if there was one person upon the earth from whom the Editor of this, and of a certain previous history, did not expect to hear again...*    Classics Pages 380

**Ayala's Angel** by *Anthony Trollope*    ISBN: *1-59462-352-X*    **$29.95**
*The two girls were both pretty, but Lucy who was twenty-one who supposed to be simple and comparatively unattractive, whereas Ayala was credited, as her Bombwhat romantic name might show, with poetic charm and a taste for romance. Ayala when her father died was nineteen...*    Fiction Pages 484

**The American Commonwealth** by *James Bryce*    ISBN: *1-59462-286-8*    **$34.45**
*An interpretation of American democratic political theory. It examines political mechanics and society from the perspective of Scotsman James Bryce*    Politics Pages 572

**Stories of the Pilgrims** by *Margaret P. Pumphrey*    ISBN: *1-59462-116-0*    **$17.95**
*This book explores pilgrims religious oppression in England as well as their escape to Holland and eventual crossing to America on the Mayflower, and their early days in New England...*    History Pages 268

QTY

**The Fasting Cure** *by Sinclair Upton*                                    ISBN: *1-59462-222-1*  **$13.95**
*In the Cosmopolitan Magazine for May, 1910, and in the Contemporary Review (London) for April, 1910, I published an article dealing with my experiences in fasting. I have written a great many magazine articles, but never one which attracted so much attention...* New Age/Self Help/Health Pages 164

**Hebrew Astrology** *by Sepharial*                                    ISBN: *1-59462-308-2*  **$13.45**
*In these days of advanced thinking it is a matter of common observation that we have left many of the old landmarks behind and that we are now pressing forward to greater heights and to a wider horizon than that which represented the mind-content of our progenitors...* Astrology Pages 144

**Thought Vibration or The Law of Attraction in the Thought World**        ISBN: *1-59462-127-6*  **$12.95**

*by William Walker Atkinson*                                               Psychology/Religion Pages 144

**Optimism** *by Helen Keller*                                        ISBN: *1-59462-108-X*  **$15.95**
*Helen Keller was blind, deaf, and mute since 19 months old, yet famously learned how to overcome these handicaps, communicate with the world, and spread her lectures promoting optimism. An inspiring read for everyone...* Biographies/Inspirational Pages 84

**Sara Crewe** *by Frances Burnett*                                    ISBN: *1-59462-360-0*  **$9.45**
*In the first place, Miss Minchin lived in London. Her home was a large, dull, tall one, in a large, dull square, where all the houses were alike, and all the sparrows were alike, and where all the door-knockers made the same heavy sound...* Childrens/Classic Pages 88

**The Autobiography of Benjamin Franklin** *by Benjamin Franklin*        ISBN: *1-59462-135-7*  **$24.95**
*The Autobiography of Benjamin Franklin has probably been more extensively read than any other American historical work, and no other book of its kind has had such ups and downs of fortune. Franklin lived for many years in England, where he was agent...* Biographies History Pages 332

Name

Email

Telephone

Address

City, State ZIP

☐ Credit Card          ☐ Check / Money Order

Credit Card Number

Expiration Date

Signature

Please Mail to:  Book Jungle
                 PO Box 2226
                 Champaign, IL 61825
or Fax to:       630-214-0564

## ORDERING INFORMATION

**web**: *www.bookjungle.com*
**email**: *sales@bookjungle.com*
**fax**: *630-214-0564*
**mail**: *Book Jungle  PO Box 2226  Champaign, IL 61825*
**or PayPal** *to sales@bookjungle.com*

*Please contact us for bulk discounts*

## DIRECT-ORDER TERMS

**20% Discount if You Order
Two or More Books**
Free Domestic Shipping!
Accepted: Master Card, Visa,
Discover, American Express

www.ingramcontent.com/pod-product-compliance
Lightning Source LLC
Chambersburg PA
CBHW080733020726
47503CB00010B/2893